BIRDIE AND THE BEASTLY DUKE

SOFI LAPORTE

http://www.sofilaporte.com

sofi@sofilaporte.com

c/o Block Services
Stuttgarter Str. 106
70736 Fellbach, Germany

Cover Art: Covers and Cupcakes

ISBN: 978-3-9505190-3-7

❀ Created with Vellum

For Maria, with Love.

CHAPTER 1

*T*he girl had been crying since York.

Sobs racked her slim body in rhythm with the mail coach's motion. She pressed a handkerchief to her face as her shoulders shook. The remaining passengers ignored the girl by looking pointedly out of the window to the rain-drenched fields, down on their books or knitting needles.

The Honourable Roberta Talbot, known to her friends as Birdie, found this intolerable. The girl's grief pierced her soul. When the tin post horn sounded, announcing their arrival at the coaching inn, Birdie decided that she would have to do something about it.

Because no one else would. Birdie to the rescue. As usual.

"Take care of the luggage, Mary," she told her maid, who'd been staring out of the window with a sour face for the last half an hour. "I'll meet you inside."

Mary pressed her lips to a thin line.

When the passengers descended, the girl followed, stumbled on the last stair, and nearly tumbled into the mud. Birdie caught her by the elbow.

"I'm sure a good cup of tea will do us both good," Birdie

chattered as she directed the girl through the rain to the inn's entrance. Warmth and the smell of food greeted them. "And some shortbread, yes? Look, they even have a good fire roaring in here." Birdie led the befuddled girl through the taproom to a table nearest to the fireplace and pushed her into a chair. Her tears had stopped, and she met Birdie's gaze with red, swollen eyes.

"What is your name, child?" Birdie asked, feeling as old as her own grandmother. She plopped down in a seat across and patted the girl's hand. Birdie had just turned twenty-one. Ages old, when one had been on the shelf before one was even out. Not that she'd ever had a chance to begin with; she felt she'd been born a crone. With a sigh, Birdie took off her soggy bonnet and wiped strands of dishevelled hair from her cheek. 'Pon her soul. She probably looked like a hag, wrapped in those shawls that made her look even plumper than she already was.

No wonder no man would look at her twice.

"Cecily," the girl whispered. "Cecily Burns." Her lips wobbled again. She swallowed, and tears filled her lovely porcelain blue eyes. With the fire flickering over her golden locks, she looked like a fairy princess. The girl was a real beauty: she had the complexion, the lithe figure, the corkscrew curls. You could curl Birdie's red hair till dooms-day, and it would stay limp and frizzy. It was her maid's bane and despair. No Milk of Roses or Olympian Dew could elim-inate the smattering of freckles on her nose. The current fashion was unfavourable for Birdie; it made her luscious figure appear plump or pregnant. She had resigned herself to all this long ago. There was nothing to be done about it.

"There, there. I'm sure it's not as bad as that. Oh, here comes the tea!" Birdie beamed at the woman who served them a tray with piping hot tea and a plate of shortbread. Her stomach growled.

"Here you go, missus," the woman muttered. Even the innkeeper's wife thought she was as old as Hera.

"Lovely." Birdie accepted the tea and biscuits with a smile. "Thank you. But I will need something more fortifying, as well. A good strong meal. What do you have?"

"We have lamb stew," the woman offered.

"Perfect. Two plates, then. With some fresh bread," Birdie replied. "We will need our rooms shortly. The rooms are aired and the fire's tended, I am sure." She beamed a smile at the woman. As the daughter of a baron who had been forced to manage her family consisting of two sisters, a wayward brother, an extravagant mother, two dogs, a parrot, and a cat, she knew how to manage her environment. Otherwise, nothing would function. Her schooldays, spent at Miss Hilversham's Seminary for Young Ladies, had seemed like a holiday in comparison. Although, even there, she'd been the girl to offer solutions to problems. Who organised the midnight picnic? Who thought of oiling the creaky door? Who prevented two girls from drowning when they fell into a well? Birdie. Always, Birdie.

"Some warm bricks in the bed will be appreciated," Birdie added. "I see you run an excellent place, here."

"Yes, ma'am." The woman straightened. "I will see to it immediately."

Turning to Cecily, Birdie said, "I'm Miss Roberta Talbot."

The girl looked at her with woeful eyes. "It *is* as bad as that," she said in a voice so quiet that Birdie hardly understood her.

Bending forward, Birdie asked, "What is?"

"You said, 'I'm sure things are not as bad as that.'" Her lips wobbled again. "But it is."

"Dear me." Birdie stirred three spoonfuls of sugar into her teacup, as usual, tasted the tea, pulled her mouth down in distaste, and added a fourth. "You shall have to tell me all about it, then."

The girl twisted her shawl in her hands. "You see. I am to be married."

Birdie's spoon stopped in a mid-stir. "You are to be congratulated?"

The girl burst into noisy tears.

"Oh dear, oh dear." Birdie set down her cup and patted her shoulders. "I suppose not." She helped wipe the girl's nose. "I take it you do *not* want to be married?"

"Oh no! It is most terrible." The girl hiccupped. "You see… you see"—she took a big gulp of breath— "I am to be married to a man I've never even met. He is hideously old. In the far north of Scotland. I don't even know exactly where." She shuddered as if it were the most horrid place imaginable.

Birdie took a big bite out of a piece of shortbread. "An arranged marriage?"

The girl shook her blonde head. She really was lovely. "I am an orphan, you see. I had a good life at the vicarage in Stanton. My father died, so the vicar and his wife took me in. They treated me like their own daughter. I was so happy there. Then a letter came." Her lips trembled once more. "I must marry a complete stranger, simply because he promised my father he would. We haven't even met. I am to go immediately to Scotland for the wedding."

Birdie looked at the girl with open mouth, a few crumbs of shortbread falling out of one corner. She found the story wildly romantic. Did the girl even know how lucky she was? She could get married. Have her own household. Be free from the constant threat of spinsterhood, and the doom, gloom and shame that came with it. She wouldn't have to work as a governess, dealing with spoiled brats, teaching them what they didn't want to learn, anyway. And Scotland! Oh, the adventure!

"My dear. That sounds utterly—" Birdie searched for a word. Something told her that "brilliant" probably wasn't a good choice.

"It is terrifying, intolerable, and utterly h-h-h-heart-breaking!" The girl sobbed again.

Suddenly Birdie understood. "Oh. You are in love with someone else."

The girl nodded into her handkerchief. "David," she said in a muffled voice. She dropped the handkerchief. Her eyes took on a feverish glow. "He is the son of the vicar who took me in. He promised he'd love me until the end of our days. We were going to tell his parents, announce our engagement, but then the letter came."

She had a man who loved her. And another man who wanted to marry her. She had *two* men who wanted her. Some girls had all the luck. Birdie felt a green snake of jealousy slither in the pit of her stomach. She clamped her hand over it. "That is unfortunate. You said this David is the son of the vicar?"

She nodded eagerly, then embarked on a detailed monologue on how wonderful her David was. Birdie nodded mechanically as she crumbled the shortbread between her fingers.

Thankfully, their bowls of stew arrived.

"Here is your supper," the landlady said. "And the rooms are ready, too."

"Wonderful." Birdie shovelled the stew into her mouth as Cecily talked. She stopped talking about David when Birdie wiped her bowl with morsels of bread. Her own bowl of stew had grown cold. Birdie wondered whether she would eat it and whether it'd be very unladylike of her to eat Cecily's bowl as well.

"I'm so sorry." There was a stricken look on Cecily's face.

"I'm only talking about myself. What about you? Are you travelling to Scotland, too?"

"I'm on the way to Newcastle. I am working as a governess. With a new family. I'm not thrilled."

"Oh! You don't want to work as a governess?"

Birdie laughed dryly. "Oh no. I'd gladly marry a stranger in the wastelands of Scotland if it meant I didn't have to be a governess. Not everyone is born a teacher, you know." She shrugged. "But some of us don't have a choice."

Cecily sat up straight. "But that's it!" She flushed with animation.

Birdie blinked. A crying Cecily had looked charming; a smiling one looked positively stunning. She was a diamond of the first water. Gentlemen in a ballroom would crowd the floor to gain her hand for a dance. Did she know that? But no. All she wanted was her David.

"What do you think?"

Birdie blinked. She'd missed what the girl said. "I'm sorry. Can you repeat that?"

"I said, then let's do it! Let's swap. Captain Eversleigh doesn't know what I look like. You go marry him, and I go in your stead as a governess! I would love to teach! I could do it, too! Newcastle isn't as far away as the north of Scotland, so I might still see David…" She clapped her hands in delight.

It was an outrageous proposition. Absolutely ridiculous. Absolutely impossible. Absolutely—

"Isn't it a splendid idea?" Cecily held her breath anxiously.

Birdie's knuckles tightened around the rim of Cecily's bowl of lamb stew.

"Absolutely."

CHAPTER 2

*B*irdie was on her way to Scotland.

Somewhere in the farthest north. She didn't even know exactly where.

She was in a private carriage that Captain Eversleigh had sent for the last stretch from Inverness to Dunross, the final destination. It was slightly more comfortable than the mail coach. At least she didn't have to share it with other passengers.

Mary, her maid, had deserted her in Inverness. She'd refused to speak to Birdie the entire trip. When the coach pulled into the last coaching inn, Mary finally opened her mouth.

"I'm taking the next coach back to London."

"But, Mary, you will not leave me? I'm sure it isn't far from here." Birdie's voice raised in pitch. She hated that there was a note of pleading in her voice.

Mary pressed her lips into a disapproving line. "What you are doing is reckless and foolhardy. If your mother ever finds out, she'll not be pleased."

Good gracious, her mother! Birdie pinched the skin at her throat in nervousness.

Mary gathered her belongings as the coach pulled to a halt. "The agreement was to accompany you to Newcastle, only," she said firmly. "I came all the way to Inverness against my good judgement. This is as far as I'm going."

Her tone indicated that no amount of bribery would change her mind. Not that Birdie had a huge amount to offer. Mary joined Birdie for some refreshment in the taproom, where she waited for the stagecoach back to London.

Because Birdie couldn't shake the feeling that she may never return to England, she wrote a last letter to her best friends Lucy, Arabella, and Pen. She handed the missive to the landlord with some coins.

"A carriage for a Miss Burns is waiting," the man grumbled as he took the letter.

Miss Burns! That was her. Birdie stepped outside and eyed the carriage with steaming black stallions.

Birdie swallowed. "That's it, then, Mary. Goodbye."

Mary nodded and handed Birdie's luggage to the hostler. "Goodbye, miss." She hesitated, and her face softened a fraction. "Godspeed."

Birdie felt a lump in her throat, and for a brief moment, she felt the urge to cling to Mary's skirts. Mary, however, showed no reluctance to leave, turned and marched back to the inn.

"Are ye comin' or no?" asked the coachman, a terrifying specimen with bushy whiskers, a black greatcoat, and a hat that shadowed his face. He held the carriage door open.

Birdie climbed up and sank into velvet cushions. The carriage set in motion and pulled out swiftly from the courtyard.

This is it, Birdie thought.

No way back.

SHE MUST HAVE SLEPT for a while. When she awoke, she saw a desolate landscape of barren heather spread out in front of her. As the carriage rattled down the road, a queasy feeling overcame her.

Burns. She was now Miss Burns. Birdie picked at her dried, flaky lips. Was it actually ethical, what she was doing? She was deceiving Cecily's fiancé.

What on earth are you doing, Roberta Charlotte Talbot? Are you completely out of your mind?

Apparently so. She hadn't thought twice when she'd jumped on Cecily Burns' offer to swap. Cecily would have arrived at the Willowburys by now, as herself.

Birdie checked her conscience. All she felt was relief that she did not have to travel to Newcastle.

She was a completely unethical person, with no conscience.

But Birdie decided she could live with that fact, if it meant that she didn't have to resign herself to her fate and lower herself to the position of governess.

"Good riddance," Birdie mumbled. She meant her job. Maybe also her conscience.

She looked out of the carriage window, where the landscape had grown increasingly desolate. Where was this place?

Raindrops pattered on the window.

Perhaps she was foolhardy, reckless and ridiculous. Mary was right; what she was doing went against every fibre of Birdie's practical nature. She'd always been the practical, reasonable one in her group of impetuous friends.

Birdie had spent some of her most wonderful years with

her friends at Miss Hilversham's Seminary for Young Ladies. They'd grown up together; they'd shared joys, trials, tears, and laughter. Then, Lucy had married a duke, Arabella's brother. Who would've thought that this would ever happen? And then Arabella had gone and married a duke as well.

In their last year, Arabella had thrown four coins into a wishing well; she wished that all four of them would marry dukes. It was, of course, a coincidence. But odd, anyhow, that a duke so conveniently came along for both their friends. Pen, poor Pen, was still at Miss Hilversham's as a student teacher. Her guardian had all but forgotten about her. And she had no other family to turn to.

She, Birdie, had a family. But by Jove, she wished she didn't. Her family was the reason she could never have a season. Her father, Baron Tottingham, had gambled their entire fortune away. That included not only her and her sisters' dowries, but the entire estate, and their house. Then he shot himself. The family moved into the dower house, the only property that still belonged to them. Her brother Freddie was now Baron Tottingham and blithely trotted in his father's footsteps. The only way to regain their fortune, he said, was to gamble even harder.

Her entire prospects, and her season, were cancelled. Instead, she had to work. She made a paltry income, which she'd sent to her family, who spent it all as soon as they received it. Then they turned to Birdie to solve their remaining problems.

"Birdie, the cost of silk has gone up and we can't afford it, but we need new gowns. What are we to do?"

"Birdie, the housekeeper is resigning because we are not paying her. Where are we to get another one?"

Birdie felt a pang of guilt as she thought of Cecily. She hadn't told her any of that. If her family ever tracked down Cecily, which they would, she wouldn't be able to tell them where exactly Birdie was. Captain Eversleigh's instructions were to "await instructions" in Inverness, meaning that Birdie was relatively safe. They would never find her there.

She pulled out the letter that Cecily had given her. It was covered in strong, masculine handwriting.

He didn't sound so bad, Birdie thought. His penmanship was legible and sensible, and he crossed his t's and dotted his i's. His name was Gabriel. A pretty name. The letter was a bit stark, granted. No-nonsense. To the point.

Dear Miss Burns,

Pray forgive the extraordinary delay of this missive, but circumstances have been such that I have been unable to contact you earlier. Whilst we have never met, our fathers were close business associates and friends who desired a union between us, believing it would be a blessing for both our families. As a captain stationed abroad, I had no opportunity to meet a suitable lady, and I acquiesced to my father's choice of a bride. However, fate intervened, and the war thrust a wedge between those plans. In the meantime, both our fathers have passed on, and my military duties have occupied me on the continent.

However, to honour the wishes of both our fathers, I am determined to remain committed to our engagement and renew my offer of my hand in marriage.

Take the mail coach to Inverness and await instructions on how to proceed from there. I will send my carriage to pick you up.

Your servant,

Gabriel Eversleigh

Birdie re-read it for the hundredth time and wondered why this Gabriel Eversleigh could not honour the engagement until now. What circumstances could he possibly mean? Better late than never, she supposed. But why not become Cecily's guardian and bequeath her a sum of money?

Probably because he didn't have any money, Birdie reasoned, as she fingered the cheap paper.

He was a captain, was he? A soldier. Cecily had said he was hideously old. Birdie suspected she might be right. He'd live in a simple hut. If she was lucky, a cottage with a garden. That would be lovely. She could raise chickens and plant bilberry bushes.

Birdie looked out of the carriage window just as it rumbled across a stone bridge. She gasped.

In front of them loomed a gigantic gothic castle.

CHAPTER 3

$\mathcal{I}$t looked like a manifestation of an eerie nightmare. Grey and monstrous, it perched on top of a cliff, as if hewn directly out of the rock. Underneath, the waves of the turbulent sea crashed into its foundation. It had countless turrets with steeples that impaled the sky like pikes. The medieval keep was a colossal, forbidding block of stone surrounded by battlements that must have been built hundreds of years ago to ward off invaders. A massive drawbridge led over a ravine where the seawater gurgled. Whoever built this fortress left nothing to chance. It must've been impossible to invade. The coach rumbled over the bridge and came to a halt in the bailey, in front of a set of stone steps leading up to the castle keep. It was an impressive block of stone, but it appeared as if someone had tried to modernise it by installing wider, more modern windows; despite this, the structure maintained its gothic style.

"Would you look at that," breathed Birdie.

No servants came running, no stable boys scurried forth to take care of the horses. The bailey was empty, and the doors and window shutters of the outer buildings were closed. Only one panel dangled from the hinges and the wind clanked with regular creaking against the wall.

Birdie climbed the stairs to the massive stone building with trepidation. The coachman had dumped her luggage in front of the massive oaken door, then climbed back onto the carriage and turned the horses.

"Wait. I thought you're Captain Eversleigh's coachman? Aren't you staying here?" Birdie called after him.

"Nay. I'm no one's coachman," he grumbled as he flicked the whip. The coach departed, rumbling over the bridge.

Birdie stood alone in the deserted bailey and blinked.

"Well. That was unanticipated." She walked up the stairs and looked at the massive door. She'd have to use both hands to lift the heavy brass knocker. She lifted it and let it slam against the door. It made a thump that echoed in the hall inside. She couldn't shake the nervous feeling that she was awakening spirits in a tomb.

"Stuff and nonsense, Birdie. Compose yourself." She wrapped her shawl tighter around her shoulders.

She hammered the knocker two more times. If no one came to open the door, she decided, she'd march around the building and find the servants' entrance. Maybe it wasn't such a bad idea to visit the kitchen first. She craved a cup of good, strong tea. And maybe some hot pie. Or good, strong beef soup. She could also do with a slice of bread and cheese, but something hot in her belly would do her good. Just as she lifted her hand for the third time, the door's hinges creaked.

Birdie jumped back.

Lo-and-behold, the vault opened. A desire to giggle rose in her chest. She bit her lips to suppress it.

The door opened, and in its shadow stood the oldest man she'd ever seen in her life.

Gracious me, now I've really awoken the dead. It flashed through her.

"You the bride?" the creature asked in a creaky voice.

Birdie snapped her mouth shut. "You the bridegroom?" she countered, somewhat louder in her surprise.

The man stared at her, his white face glinting in the shadows. He opened his mouth and bared a set of yellowed teeth, uttering a noise that was unidentifiable.

Birdie backed off, alarmed.

With a jolt, she realised that the noise must be laughter.

It sounded like wood creaking.

The man attempted to lift her suitcase.

"Perhaps you should leave it," Birdie said. It looked like the man was going to break in half simply by lifting her luggage.

"Get in," he replied. He'd somehow managed to pick up all three pieces of her luggage without collapsing.

Birdie stepped over the threshold into the hall. A cold draft of air blew about her. Then the door closed behind her with a thump, and she was swallowed by darkness.

Birdie stood in a hall that seemed to have appeared right out of the time of medieval warlords. A massive stone fireplace was carved into one end of the hall, and a long wooden table stretched across the entire room. A staircase at the end of the hall led to the upper floors. Elaborate tapestries that would put the tapestry of Bayeux to shame hung on the walls.

"Goodness me. I've never seen anything like it," Birdie mumbled and rubbed her hands. She shivered in the cold.

"Follow me," the creature said as he shuffled to the stairs. He went up slowly, step by step. Birdie was behind him, impatient and worried that he'd collapse under his burden at any moment. He stumbled over the last stair and Birdie caught him by the elbow.

"Isn't there another servant here who can help with the luggage?" she asked.

"Eh?" He turned his head and squinted at her.

"Isn't there someone else who can carry the luggage?" Birdie raised her voice.

"Yes, yes. He must marry the baggage," the man muttered and shuffled on.

"No. I meant—" Birdie interrupted herself as they reached a tremendous corridor.

She gulped. It looked dark, dusty—and definitely haunted. "Stuff and nonsense," she whispered to herself. The man had shuffled on and halted in front of a room.

"Here." He nodded at the door.

"Wait, allow me." Birdie walked to him and opened the door so that he didn't have to put down the luggage. "Oh!" she exclaimed.

She hadn't expected such a lovely room. All gothic oak and with velvet blue drapes over the bed and the window. The window! Birdie ran over to it. She had a striking view of the ocean. It was dark grey and turbulent; impossible to tell where the water ended and the clouds began. "How utterly marvellous!" She gasped.

The man dropped off the luggage by her bed and shuffled back to the door.

"Wait! I take it you're not the, er, bridegroom. Who are you? And where is Captain Eversleigh?"

"Eh?" The man leaned forward and cupped a hand over his ear. "You have to talk louder, miss."

"Who. Are. You?" Birdie roared into his ear.

He snapped to attention, pulling himself up to his full height as if suddenly remembering who he was.

"Higgins. Higgins at your service, miss," he said in an unexpectedly clear voice. "I am the butler." He stared at her and blinked. "And you're the bride."

Well. They'd already established that, hadn't they?

"Higgins. Where is Captain Eversleigh?"

"The wedding is tomorrow morning at ten. In the chapel," Higgins replied, ignoring her question. He turned and left the room.

"Wait. Higgins!" She went after him in the corridor. "May I have some tea? Or supper?"

But the butler had all but disappeared.

"Now this won't do at all." Birdie frowned. She hadn't eaten since that sloppy breakfast at the coaching inn early this morning, which had consisted of a thin gruel and an even thinner mug of tea. They hadn't stopped at any other inn, since there wasn't any on the way, the coachman had explained.

Her stomach growled. It must be reaching suppertime, Birdie conjectured. She squinted down the dusky corridor and rubbed her arms.

"There's got to be a kitchen somewhere," she said aloud.

KITCHENS WERE USUALLY on the lower floors. She'd run into a domestic eventually, she figured, then she could ask them for some supper.

She wrapped herself in a shawl, took a candle and lit it, for it was getting dark rapidly, and ventured forth.

Goodness me. Wouldn't her friend Lucy love this? And Pen, with whom she'd shared a room at Miss Hilversham's seminary. And Arabella, who was always so proper, duke's daughter that she was, but one who'd thirsted for adventure as much as any of them. She felt a wave of nostalgia sweep over her. What wouldn't she give to be with them now? No corner of the castle would be safe with them beside her.

Birdie sighed so loudly; it echoed along the corridor, giving her a fright.

"You really have to stop this," she scolded herself and pressed a hand over her thudding heart. "Ghosts. Fustian."

She was in the main hall. Shouldn't the big oaken table be set for dinner by now? But there was no fire burning in the fireplace, and the table wasn't set. She went to the main door and tried to open it.

It was locked. A pang of alarm shot through her. Why was the door locked?

"Hello? Higgins? Captain Eversleigh? Is anyone here?" Her voice echoed through the hall.

No answer.

Was Eversleigh even in residence? It looked like not. How excessively odd. Why had he wanted her to come to this castle when he wasn't here himself? Was he away? Would he arrive in the morning?

"Very well, Roberta Talbot. You can do one of two things. One, panic. Two—" she gulped—"find that kitchen and get yourself something to eat. Which is it to be?"

Her stomach growled in response.

In the end, she found the kitchen by accident. As she returned to the stairs, she spotted a small door in the wall to her right. She opened it. It revealed a smaller set of stairs winding itself down. Servants' stairs.

"This must be it," Birdie muttered. Thankful that she'd brought the candle along, she followed the stairs down.

She found herself standing in what must have been the servants' hall. The kitchen, however, was empty.

"Looks like you have to prepare your own supper." If there was one thing Birdie knew how to do, it was cooking. She'd spent countless hours in the kitchen of her former home, watching their cook dice, boil, broil, chop, and whisk everything from Yorkshire puddings and mutton cutlets to minced pies and madeira tartlets. Cook's biscuits were legendary. When Cook was in a good mood, she'd sometimes allowed her to help cut out the biscuits and stamp emblems on the dough with the biscuit stamp. But most of the time, whilst she tolerated Birdie's presence, she did not approve of her helping in the kitchen.

She'd put her hands against her hips, purse her lips and say, "You're a baron's daughter, miss. It's beneath your station to be here. I'll let you watch, but you won't move a finger, you won't." Then she'd explain in great detail how to broil a good lamb.

Birdie was grateful for every minute she was allowed to spend in the kitchens. It was her way of avoiding her family whenever she visited: her mother, whom she could never please, her two sisters, whom she did not understand, and her brother, who was a rake and a gambler and perpetually absent.

When she was younger, Birdie sometimes thought that she must've been a changeling, swapped at birth, for she had nothing at all in common with her family. All her mother's beauty and ethereal loveliness had gone to her sisters. Her mother had lamented that Birdie was plump, with devil's hair and street-boy freckles. Once, her mother had forced her to eat chalk, hoping it would whiten up her skin. She'd had to scrub her face with freckle wash, a mixture of lemon, milk and brandy, which left her skin raw and irritated. She wasn't allowed to go outside, for she had to stay out of the sun.

It was a relief when her holiday time at her home was over and she could return to Miss Hilversham's seminary, where no one cared about the colour of her hair or how many freckles she had. She considered the seminary to be her real home. There, too, she'd wheedled the cook to teach her a thing or two about whipping up a good syllabub.

Birdie set the candle down on the centre table and lit a lamp.

The kitchen had a surprisingly modern cast-iron range,

which looked unused, as well as a range of copper cookware, pots and pans in the shelves.

She studied the larder, which, to her surprise, contained some food items, predominantly oats and flour, but also a basket full of eggs and blood sausages that hung from hooks. In a drawer, she found some stale bread.

"Let's see. Sausages. Eggs. Bread. Hm. Not the freshest, but it'll do." She lit the stove and prepared her supper.

CHAPTER 4

*H*e'd seen her arrive earlier.

He'd observed from his window in the tower room how the coach rattled over the drawbridge and stopped in the bailey. He'd seen her emerge from the coach, wrapped in what appeared to be countless layers of shawls. He'd seen her wait for a footman who never came and watch as the coachman unloaded the luggage unceremoniously in the yard. Then the coach left. The girl in the shawls remained behind, looking around helplessly until she marched up the stairs decisively and hammered on the door. So, that was Miss Cecily Burns.

He'd given Higgins orders to bring the girl to the room. He hadn't forgotten about supper, had he? Higgins was a loyal soul, but he really was getting rather old.

He sighed.

He felt the girl's presence in the castle almost viscerally. She'd changed the entire atmosphere. When was the last time a woman had set foot in this place? The old Duke hadn't spent too much time here, and his wife had passed away when she was young.

Gabriel turned away from the window. He froze.

"Is anyone here?" the voice echoed faintly. What was she doing in this part of the castle? Didn't he tell Higgins to put her in the old duchess' room on the other side?

Dash it, Higgins had left and forgotten the supper after all. Now what to do?

He cursed under his breath.

He'd promised his father he'd honour the engagement to Burns' daughter, and by Jove, he'd do that if it was the last thing he'd ever do, even if it went against every fibre of his being. He felt black despair course through him. It had been the last thing his father had asked of him. The girl's own father had passed away with the smallpox. She would be destitute unless he honoured the engagement. "Do the right thing, I beg of you, son." He'd read his father's letter before he charged into battle. Before chaos broke out and he'd come close to death; not knowing that, at that very moment, his father was lying on his deathbed.

He'd forgotten all about the promise and the letter until he'd found the crumpled sheet of paper in the inner pocket of his old military coat. The ink was barely legible, and the paper was splattered with blood and mud. It had taken him months to find Miss Burns. He'd almost given up the quest of finding her, when, to his surprise, the vicar of a small town in Yorkshire had written to him that, indeed, he cared for the orphaned and destitute Miss Cecily Burns. So now he had to marry her.

It had been his father's last request. He'd sworn to himself he'd honour it at all costs. But if the lady was reluctant to wed him, and well she should, there was nothing he could do.

Gabriel took a shaky breath.

He'd marry the girl tomorrow. Then he'd have paid his dues and would be relieved from it all.

The plan was to meet her then. Should he be a gentleman and greet her now? It would be the right thing to do.

He'd rather not, though.

He broke out in a sweat. Coward!

Yet he had to make sure she was taken care of.

He went to her room. He knocked. No one replied. He lifted his hand to the latch, hesitated, then pressed it down.

The room was empty. Where the deuce was she?

The smell of fried sausages suddenly permeated the air. Was Higgins frying sausages?

He stealthily descended the stairs to the main hall, before turning to the stairs to the servants' hall.

There she was.

Standing by the stove. Frying sausages.

He was so stunned he nearly gave away his presence. He peered around the corner.

He saw her turn and tilt the contents of the pan onto a plate. She took the plate and lantern, carried both to the table in the servants' hall, sat down and ate like there was no tomorrow. His stomach grumbled.

Suddenly, she paused with the fork halfway to her mouth and stared in his direction. He pressed himself against the cold stone wall.

"Hello? Is anyone there?" she called out. When there came no reply, the girl sighed. "I swear there is someone watching me. Bah, what a creepy place this is! I warn you, whoever you are: ghoul, ghost, gnome or poltergeist, don't cross my path! I refuse to faint or be afraid. In fact, I don't faint. I couldn't even if I tried. Now go back to your coffin, crypt or whatever unhallowed ground you ventured forth from. Because I am not amused. Especially when I'm hungry. Dear me, I'm hungry." She bit into the sausage with gusto. "Hm. This is good."

It looked like his bride not only had a good appetite but also a head full of common sense.

This, he decided, wasn't bad at all.

He crept back up the stairs whence he'd come from, stunned. He nearly stumbled on the top stair, giving himself away. Coward, he scolded himself again, as he returned to his room.

BIRDIE WAS LOST.

With only the lantern to show her the way, she'd ventured into a chain of corridors, taken a right turn instead of a left, and ended up in a series of dusty rooms, where the furniture was draped by holland covers. One thing was clear to her: this place was empty; there wasn't a single soul in the entire castle. Not even a ghost. It was entirely dark, with only occasional rays of moonlight flitting through the grime-smeared windows.

She hadn't come this way before; she thought uneasily, as she shifted the lantern from one hand to the other. She remembered coming down a winding staircase, and there was a stone staircase right there, except it was to her left, when it should have been to her right. On the other hand, maybe it was correct, and she'd simply been too hungry to pay proper attention when she'd come this way earlier.

Birdie pushed the heavy oaken door open and climbed the stairs.

Dear me, those stairs never seemed to end. She should be coming out in the main hall. Why did she have the feeling she was climbing a tower?

She'd recently read a book of brand-new fairy tales written by German brothers named Grimm, translated to English. One story, called "Rapunzel", was about a girl with long hair, who was walled up in a tower. The Brothers

Grimm must have envisioned a tower like this. Without the stairs.

Reaching the top, she found her way barred by another door. Through the gap between the door and the stone floor, she saw glimmers of light. Someone was in the room. Was this where Higgins slept?

Relieved to finally find another living soul within these walls, she pushed the door open.

She found herself in a round tower room, with only a weak fire in the fireplace that barely lit up half of the room, leaving the other half in the dark. She made out a bed and an armchair in front of the fire. But no one was there.

A storm howled around the tower, and the wind rattled against the small window.

"How excessively odd," she mumbled, lifting her lantern.

Then she heard it. A scraping coming from the fireplace. From the armchair, the back of which faced her.

Birdie's mouth dried up, and her heart hammered painfully in her chest.

A dark shadow unfolded itself from the armchair, growing to tremendous proportions. The shadowy figure grew, nearly touching the roof beams. Orange tongues flickered about it, hissing, spitting like the flames of hell.

Goodness, there were phantoms in this place, after all.

"Away with you, you ghoul!" she screamed and threw her lamp at it. She squeezed her eyes shut to cut off the terrifying vision. She stumbled backwards, down the stairs, half falling, half crawling, scraping her knees, getting up again, and running down the corridor. Somehow, she found her room. Gasping, she threw the door shut and drew the bolt.

For good measure, she pushed her dresser in front of the door.

Then she crawled into bed, drew the blankets and pillows over her head. Eventually, she fell into an exhausted sleep.

CHAPTER 5

*B*irdie overslept.

Considering that she was all alone in a musty, and very much haunted, castle, she hadn't slept that badly.

When she awoke, it was mid-morning, and she sat up straight in her bed. Now, in the morning light, last night seemed like an exaggerated nightmare, and she was almost angry at herself for having given in to panic.

Ghouls and ghosts indeed.

She should've investigated the creature, asked it some questions. She could've learned something about the afterlife. Or maybe she could've helped break its curse. Instead, she'd run faster than a chicken about to be slaughtered.

But what was even more likely was that there probably had been nothing to begin with. Higgins must've lit the fireplace. It must've been shadows cast on the wall by the flames.

Her nerves had been frayed. She'd been lost. She was exhausted and confused. It must have been her mind playing tricks on her.

Whatever that had been, she had other, more immediate things to worry about.

It was her wedding day.

Her stomach emitted an unladylike growl.

"And of course, no one thought to bring me breakfast," she grumbled. She wasn't about to repeat her activity from last night, however. She intended to be the lady of the castle, not the cook.

"Ten o'clock. Didn't this Higgins say the wedding is in the chapel at ten o'clock?" She pulled out her pocket watch and shrieked. It was a quarter to ten. She had to get ready, and it very much seemed that no maid was here to help her.

Birdie scrambled into a clean, but crumpled, blue dress, pulled back her frizzy hair in a loose bun and squashed her spectacles on her nose. Then she pushed the dresser away from the door. She drew on a coat, grabbed her bonnet, and left the room.

The front door in the hall was unlocked.

She pushed it open and stood in the bailey, looking around her with narrowed eyes. A raindrop fell on her nose. Higgins had said the wedding would be in the church.

What church? Where?

Did he mean that little building beyond, nestled between two outer buildings; the one with a small steeple that could pass as a chapel?

She walked across the courtyard towards the building and pushed the door open.

She narrowed her eyes in the sudden dark and discerned four figures inside. Finally, some living beings!

Her heart thudding, she walked down the aisle, wondering which one was Captain Eversleigh.

There was, undeniably, Higgins' spindly figure. There was a reverend, who stood in front of the altar, recognisable in his black double-breasted cassock, gown and cap. A man in rough clothes, looking like a farm's hand, stood in the front, turning his battered hat in his hands. She looked at him doubtfully. That couldn't be Captain Eversleigh, could it?

Her eyes wandered over to the fourth man, who was sitting hunched in a pew, half in shadow.

"I'm sorry I'm late," Birdie said breathlessly, as she stumbled down the aisle.

The seated figure detached itself from the shadows and rose as she approached.

"Miss Cecily Burns," he said in the deepest voice she'd ever heard. "I am Gabriel Eversleigh."

At that moment, thunder clapped, and lightning flashed, illuminating the horrifying figure of the creature who stood before her.

Birdie screamed.

AWAY. Away! She stumbled outside, running through the bailey. Rain pelted down, and lightning flashed in the blackened sky.

She ran across the drawbridge. The wood was wet, and she skidded, slid, rotated both arms, and fell face long into the mud. She remained lying there, completely stunned.

A monster.

He was a monster!

It was that creature from the tower. A creature of shadow and fire, a phantom. She hadn't imagined it at all. The same fearful height, the same shadow, the same gleaming pale face. That was Captain Eversleigh?

Rain poured down and thunder rattled through the sky, and drummed on her face, in biting ice-cold little stabs. Oddly enough, that calmed her down.

There are no such things as monsters.

But she'd clearly seen it.

That figure, dark and tall, dressed entirely in black. He'd risen and turned. He'd looked perfectly normal on one side, with a profile of a sensuous mouth and a proud Grecian nose. He was almost dashing, in fact—then he'd turned his head, and his face emerged from the darkness.

It was completely disfigured. It'd been the stark contrast that had startled her so. One half was beautiful, the other—

Oh, dear sweet heaven. She clapped her hands over her face. The other side was as though it had melted away. There was a black hole where the eye was supposed to be. She hadn't seen more because she'd screamed like a banshee and fled.

Birdie hadn't even known she could scream like that.

She sat in the mud and allowed the rain to wash over her. Closing her eyes, lifting her head toward the sky, she came to a conclusion.

"Roberta Charlotte Talbot. You ought to be completely and utterly ashamed of yourself." She struggled up and marched right back.

WHY WAS HE SURPRISED? He shouldn't have expected anything different. The girl had taken half a look at him, screamed and fled from his sight. For the second time.

He sighed.

Yesterday, she'd suddenly stood in his tower room, her hair flowing about her, holding a candle, looking like an apparition for all that was worth. He'd blinked, certain that he was seeing visions. He'd risen from his armchair and had been about to open his mouth to say something when she'd hissed "ghoul!" and thrown her lantern at him. She'd nearly set the entire place on fire.

He'd been certain Miss Burns wouldn't come to the

wedding. After yesterday, he'd been certain she'd pack her bags and leave before dawn broke. He must have frightened her out of her wits. He'd been too cowardly to go after her to see whether she was alright. If he'd done so, he'd probably have terrified her even more. Not that it mattered, because he had managed to do that this morning.

He'd never been vain or concerned about his looks. When he'd woken up in the field hospital and found half his face burnt and his left eye gone, he'd taken it with resignation.

Others were worse off. Others had lost their limbs. Some not one, but both. More than one fellow had lost his arms as well. What did it matter if one no longer looked handsome when others had lost their lives? But he hadn't counted on people's reactions towards him. How they averted their eyes with embarrassment. The disgust, or even fear showing on their faces.

By Jove, that scream. His hand shook as he took out a handkerchief to wipe his brow. He'd heard many screams in the many battles he'd fought. Yet he'd never heard a scream of such stark, utter terror. She was, of course, entirely right to run. No one in her right mind ought to marry him, least of all an innocent daughter of one of his father's friends. He wasn't doing the poor girl any favours at all. What was he thinking?

Reverend McAloy cleared his throat and snapped his bible shut. "I take it there's to be no wedding today?"

"No," Gabriel said through gnashed teeth.

But, at that moment, the church doors opened for a second time.

Lightning flashed, illuminating a figure in dark blue. Her hair, a vibrant red, poured over her shoulders. She looked like a fairy queen.

Caked in mud from head to toe.

Gabriel blinked. By George. She'd returned.

"Excuse me," she said breathlessly after she came down the aisle, her nose high in the air. "I had to quickly—you know."

"Eh?" Higgins tilted his head.

"You had to, what?" The reverend stared at her in astonishment, clutching his bible as if to ward off a spirit.

She waved a hand. "You know." She bent forward and hissed. "The chamber pot."

The reverend flushed beet red. "Oh. Of course."

Gabriel was dumbfounded.

Then she lifted her hand, hesitatingly, and prodded his arm. "I just need to make sure you're real." He felt her finger poke into his jacket. "That you're not a phantom."

"I am not a phantom," he rasped. But maybe that was a lie. He'd lived the life of a ghost since that blasted war.

"I don't believe you are, now. I was somewhat out of my depth last night. With the storm and all." She stared fully into his face.

He flinched and averted his face.

Then he froze and willed himself not to look away; to let her see every inch. Every badly healed scar, every discoloured lesion. She needed to see what she was marrying.

She looked pale, but she did not look away. She pushed the mud-splattered spectacles further up her stubby nose, spectacles that were simply too big for her, making her hazel eyes look owlish. Freckles dusted her nose. Or maybe it was mud, for there were splatters on her milk-white cheek and neck. Her full pink lips were pursed.

She barely reached his shoulders. She was the prettiest thing he'd ever seen, mud and all.

"Does it hurt, still?" she asked.

"Only if exposed to extreme heat or cold. The skin there is sensitive." His hand went up to rub the scar on his cheek.

Birdie nodded. "Rubbing almond oil and lemon juice on it might help."

He was speechless.

The reverend grumbled. "Shall we proceed, now? Or do we spend the remaining morning here discussing treatments against scars?"

"Are you certain you want to marry me?" Gabriel heard himself ask huskily. He still couldn't believe she'd actually returned.

The girl nodded.

A loud snore interrupted the conversation.

Higgins. He sat hunched over in the first pew and slept soundly.

"By all means, get on with it." Gabriel turned to the rector.

"Dearly beloved, we are gathered here together in the sight of God…"

The reverend droned on, and Gabriel could barely focus on his words. He was only aware of the girl next to him, shivering, now and then sending him a sideways look of trepidation.

The reverend reached the concluding statement: "Wilt thou love her, comfort her, honour, and keep her in sickness and in health; and, forsaking all other, keep thee only unto her, so long as ye both shall live?"

He heard himself say, as if in a dream, "I will."

McAloy, satisfied, turned to the girl. "Wilt thou obey him, and serve him, love, honour and—"

"Wait."

What now?

"Why does he get to love me, and I have to obey and serve him?" Her words echoed in the church. "It's not entirely fair, is it?"

The reverend blinked as his mouth dropped open.

Gabriel never thought he'd be capable of being speechless more than twice an hour, but there it was.

The reverend sighed. "These are the words of the Book of Common Prayer which you must repeat." He attempted to speak in a patient, slow kind of way that one assumed when one was talking to recalcitrant children.

"But I don't quite see why the loving part is limited to men only and the obeying part to women." There was a stubborn tilt to her lower lip.

"My dear, this isn't quite the time to debate—"

"Very well." Gabriel's voice sounded harsher than intended. Everyone fell quiet immediately. "I will repeat the vows, shall I? *I will love you, comfort you, honour and—obey and serve you—as long as we both shall live.*"

McAloy scratched his head. "Not sure this is quite the thing." He looked for help to the witnesses, but Higgins was still snoring, and the other man lifted his shoulders dismissively.

"Proceed. And skip the part on the duties of man and wife. That is a command." Eversleigh's voice sounded like a whiplash. McAloy winced and proceeded. Throwing a cowering look at him, he added the words, "Wilt thou love him" to her vow.

She gave him a hard look. "I will." Her voice rang firmly in the church.

Gabriel felt something odd lodge in his chest. For some inexplicable reason, he felt like weeping.

Then everyone was looking at him.

"You have to take my hand." She had a sweet voice.

Her hand was cold and small in his, which was huge and rough. It twitched at first, then lay quietly like a bird in his scarred palm.

The ring was too big. She'd have to wear it on her forefinger for now. He'd have to ask the blacksmith to make it smaller.

"… I pronounce that they be man and wife." McAloy wiped his forehead. "Congratulations, Your Grace. Now, to sign the register."

Gabriel still held her hand and was reluctant to let it go. With his other, he pulled out his handkerchief.

"Come here."

She threw him a wary look. Blast her. Was she going to be forevermore afraid of him?

He lifted his hand. She flinched. Dropping her hand, he held her chin and gently tilted her face to him.

He wiped the mud off her cheek.

Her eyes widened as if this was the most unexpected thing he had done this entire day.

"There," he said, gruffly. He was thoroughly ruffled.

"Your Grace. The signature."

He turned to the altar and scribbled his signature on the parchment.

The girl fiddled with her spectacles and bent over the paper.

She scribbled an illegible signature. Then she froze and pointed with the quill at the paper.

"It says, Gabriel Eversleigh, the Duke of Dunross. That can't be right?" Her voice was high-pitched.

"Of course it's right. This is His Grace, the Duke of Dunross. And you're Her Grace, the Duchess of Dunross now." The reverend took the book.

"You're a—a—duke?" It sounded like an accusation. Her hazel eyes widened in shock.

"What if I am?" Why did he say it in such bloody defensive way? Granted, he hadn't wanted to inherit the title, but there was no reason to hide it, either. He knew he should've signed the letter as a duke, but had been reluctant to do so.

To his alarm, he saw her face drain of all colours.
She sobbed and laughed simultaneously.
This alarmed him even more.
"If only Arabella knew!" She sighed.
Then she crumpled to the floor.

CHAPTER 6

*B*irdie awoke lying on a threadbare sofa in the great hall. She was wrapped in a thick, woollen plaid, feeling warm and drowsy. A fire roared in the massive fireplace across from her.

Crikey. She hadn't fainted, had she? She never fainted. And if she did, how had she ended up here? Had *he* carried her?

"No, Higgins, I asked, did you take up her bags, not, did she eat haggis." That was his voice. Deep and harsh. Birdie shuddered.

Had she really just married him? She'd dreamed he was a duke.

"Yes, Your Grace," Higgins replied. "Haggis we have to order down at the village. Do you want me to get some? We have porridge now for the wedding breakfast."

Your Grace. She hadn't dreamt it. She'd married the phantom in the tower. Oh dear, what had she done?

She turned her head and watched as Higgins shuffled towards the suit of armour next to the staircase. Eversleigh reacted quickly, took the man by his shoulders, and gently led him to the left, to prevent a collision. "The door is here. Hold on to the rail so you don't fall. The stairs down are tricky."

Birdie turned over on the sofa to see where they were, bumped into a side table next to it and toppled over an oil lamp. It clattered to the stone floor.

Immediately, the men fell silent.

"Sorry," Birdie mumbled. It hadn't been lit, so there was no harm done.

"Miss Burns. Er." The man she'd married not an hour ago cleared his throat. Clearly, he did not know how to address his new wife. "Cecily?"

Birdie swallowed. "Birdie, please." She squinted at him. The man had retreated into the shadows. Where were her glasses? She saw something glint on the table in front of her. There they were. Relieved, she pushed them up her nose. She still couldn't see him any clearer, because he'd retreated even further into the shadows. There was not much light coming through the stained-glass windows from above.

"Birdie?"

"M—my friends call me that." Now would've been an appropriate moment for her to confess that she'd swapped places with the real Cecily. Yet she felt oddly reluctant to do so. "Did someone mention wedding breakfast?" She looked around for Higgins, who was setting the table rather noisily, dropping the plates and cups randomly on the table.

"There is some porridge, Higgins says." Her husband looked like he was about to flee. Was the man frightened of her? How curious.

Birdie pulled out a rickety chair from the table and sat down.

"Well? Aren't you going to join me?" Birdie pointed to the place across from her. She caught Higgins' hand just in time before he poured the tea right into the bowl of porridge instead of the teacup.

"Thank you, Higgins, I can take it from here." Birdie took the teapot from his skeletal hand.

"You want beer?" He squinted at her. "For breakfast?"

Birdie choked back a laugh. "No. Tea is fine." She shook her head, and Higgins shuffled away, mumbling, "Beer she wants. For her wedding breakfast. What has this world come to."

Tea, tea, my kingdom for a cup of tea. At least it smelled properly strong. Birdie took a sip and nearly spat it out again. It was the strongest tea she'd ever had in her entire life, pitch black and so bitter it burned her tongue. She topped her cup up with milk and added four spoons of sugar.

Her husband approached cautiously and sat down at the farthest end of the table. At this distance, they couldn't properly converse; they'd have to shout at each other.

Without much ado, Birdie picked up her cup and wandered down to the other side of the table and sat down closer to him.

He clearly didn't feel comfortable with this and edged away from his seat.

He's a creature of shadows, it crossed through her mind.

From here, the fire flickered over his face, and she could make out the wounded side of his face.

Now that she had the comfort of warm liquid in her stomach and had got over the excitement of her wedding, she could've kicked herself.

It was merely a very bad burn. Some scars were thick and bulky, others red and blue. It didn't look pretty. Scars were scars. But it wasn't as monstrous as she'd first thought. Where she'd initially thought he had a hole for an eye was a black eyepatch. In the church, she hadn't seen the covering; it had looked like the gaping eyehole of a skull. He had a bit of a pirate-like look about him. It made him look quite dashing. He also wasn't old at all. She guessed him to be in his mid-thirties, at the most.

Birdie sipped her tea thoughtfully.

"Haven't you had your eyeful of me yet?" he ground out.

Birdie flushed. "I apologise if I'm being rude." She looked away, but her eyes found their way back to his face again immediately. It was odd how she found it impossible to look away.

To distract herself, she got up, fetched two bowls of porridge, poured milk and sugar over them and placed one in front of him. A peace offering.

The porridge was lumpy and half cold, but it was better than nothing.

"Who is Arabella?"

She looked at him with enormous eyes. "Arabella?"

"You said, before you fainted, 'If only Arabella knew.'"

She fiddled with her spectacles. Under no circumstances would she tell her new husband, a duke, the silly story of the wishing well.

"She is a childhood friend of mine, now the Duchess of Morley. For some reason, Arabella desired all her friends to marry dukes." Birdie shrugged and played with her cup. "She herself is the daughter of a duke, so perhaps it was natural for her to think along those lines. I, myself, never really cared much about it." That was a half-truth. She'd not particularly cared about dukes, but she did want to get married and have her own family, her very own home. She had dreamed about it for as long as she could remember.

"Why did you return?" her husband asked abruptly.

Birdie stirred her porridge, carefully weighing her next words. After a moment of reflection, she decided to tell him the truth. "Because it was raining, and I had no place to go. I realised my reaction was overly exaggerated, that you clearly weren't a phantom, and that I wanted to get married. Very much so."

He looked taken aback. "Why?"

Why did a girl want to get married? Wasn't that self-evident? "Independence," she replied. "A married woman is freer than an unmarried one. I never enjoyed being a spinster. Existing at the charity of others. If you marry, you have your own household in which you can be in charge. Even if it's just deciding what's for supper."

"You could've married someone else."

Birdie uttered an involuntary laugh.

"I fail to understand what is so amusing." The man's black eyebrows came together in a scowl.

"It is simple. No one would have me. I have nothing to offer. Neither prospects, dowry, nor, alas, beauty." Birdie pulled at a bedraggled lock of hair that hung limply down her face. She still had mud stuck in her hair. She looked candidly into her husband's face. "And, as it turns out, you're a duke. A somewhat eccentric one who seems to live the life of a hermit, but a duke, nonetheless. That's not such a bad catch."

"But you didn't know I was a duke when you returned." He emphasised the word 'duke' as if this seemed to matter to him.

"No, I didn't. It came as a surprise." She stirred her porridge slowly. She wondered whether Cecily would've liked to marry him after all, had she known he was a duke.

Her husband sighed. "I inherited the dukedom unexpectedly from a very remote relative. So distant, that the 'relative' is not even applicable. I had no idea there was such a title in my family. But it turned out there was, and he had no issue. So, I inherited." He shrugged dismissively.

Birdie propped an elbow on the table. It all sounded wildly romantic.

"You inherited the castle and the title and the grounds. That's rather fantastic. That doesn't happen too often to people."

His harsh laughter made her jump.

"I inherited more debt than anything else. This pile of stone here, and another degenerated estate further south. But never fear. My captain's pension yields sufficient funds to take care of a wife."

"So, what is going to happen next?" she asked conversationally. He still had not touched his bowl. Was he ever going to eat that?

"Next?"

"Yes. What happens now?"

"You finish your porridge, get back in the carriage and return to where you came from."

Birdie dropped her spoon in the bowl with a clank.

"But we're only just married!"

"Yes. Thank you for reminding me of that incontrovertible fact. I had all but forgotten." His voice was dry.

"I don't understand."

He fiddled with something underneath the table and then thumped a heavy-looking velvet pouch before her. The contents inside clinked.

"What is this?" Birdie raised a perplexed eyebrow.

"Your allowance. You will receive this amount per annum from now on. You can do with it as you wish."

"That is supremely generous of you, but—" Birdie shook her head. "You mentioned you wanted me to leave. Or did I misunderstand?"

He nodded tersely. "The condition is that you return to the vicarage. You may also stay at Sandmoore Hall, but I have been informed that it is in worse shape than this place here. London is another alternative. My father's townhouse."

Birdie pressed her fingers against her temple. "You are sending me away? This marriage is to be in name only?"

"Precisely."

"You think that by marrying me,"––or rather Cecily–– "you are fulfilling your promise, and you can simply dismiss me? I am your wife! What kind of promise-keeping is that?"

A faint blush covered the healthy part of his cheek.

"It is the only way for me to honour both our fathers' wishes and take care of you, while simultaneously ensuring that you are not imprisoned here. You are free to go."

"Imprisoned," echoed Birdie. "I find it rather difficult to understand your train of thought."

"You will have nothing to do with all this here." Eversleigh gestured to the medieval hallway around them. "You can lead a trouble-free existence elsewhere. Return to your father's town, if you wish. Or set up house in London. As Duchess of Dunross, all doors will be open to you. My pension won't allow for a lavish lifestyle, but it's sufficient for you to enjoy the season. Take lovers. I don't care what you do with your life, as long as you leave me in peace here."

Birdie's mouth dropped open.

He wanted to get rid of her, did he? Well, he hadn't counted on the stubbornness of Birdie.

"I think I shan't," she said, in a quiet but firm tone. "I think I'd like to stay here." As she cleaned out her porridge bowl, she added, "I'd prefer to be properly married. With a proper family that comes with it. Children and all that." She reached for his bowl. If he wasn't going to eat it, then she would.

CHAPTER 7

*G*abriel Eversleigh, Duke of Dunross, found himself in an odd situation.

He'd married a girl and had expected her to leave right after the wedding.

Except she didn't want to.

Maybe he shouldn't find that so surprising, since they'd been married for not even three hours. When one married, the wife, under normal circumstances, tended to stay. For life. That was commonly accepted to be the purpose of marriage.

She'd said that she wanted children. Sweet, pudgy babies that smelled of milk and sunshine. That would cling to his legs and call him Papa. Then they would grow up and go to war and kill and get killed.

He got up so quickly that the chair toppled over and crashed to the ground.

"Never."

The girl looked up from her bowl, surprised. A smear of porridge stuck at the corner of her mouth. "Never?" she echoed dumbly.

"This whole thing, this whole marriage, is only to fulfil a vow, to take care of you. Nothing more."

"And what about your vow to me? You made it barely two hours ago." Her eyes bore into his. He felt himself breaking out in a sweat. She'd made him say it, hadn't she?

"*To love and honour him 'til death do us part...*" she whispered the words as he recalled them in his memory. "That is a very serious vow to make." She propped her elbow on the table. "I think that vow supersedes the one you made earlier. It encompasses the previous vow as well."

Love. There it was again. She'd not only made him take a vow of love, but she insisted he kept it.

It was insupportable.

Mumbling something unintelligible, Gabriel backed away, hit his legs on the stairs, and stumbled up the staircase.

"We can discuss this later if you want," he heard her call after him. "Are you going to be here for luncheon?" He grabbed hold of the bannister and hauled himself up three steps at a time.

Away.

Away from her.

She had to leave immediately.

WELL.

That had been the oddest conversation in her entire life.

Birdie looked down at her bowl. And that had been the horridest porridge she'd ever had, even if she'd ended up eating two bowls. The cold porridge sat like a stone in her stomach. Clearly, the cook wasn't the best. The poor meal lowered her spirits. Or perhaps she was feeling rather upset about the conversation she'd just had.

If she was going to be duchess here, she was going to have

to do something about the lack of servants, the degenerate state of the entire place, and the food––most definitely, the food.

Suddenly, Higgins appeared in front of her. Birdie jumped in her seat.

"Higgins." She pressed her hand on her racing heart. "You gave me a fright."

"I have brought the beer, Your Grace," the man said.

"Thank you, Higgins, but I won't be needing it."

He set the tankard down in front of her regardless and remained standing next to her chair.

"Is there anything else, Higgins?" Birdie asked.

"The carriage is here, Your Grace."

"Send it away."

He shuffled away, nodding. "Tell it to stay."

That wasn't exactly what she'd said, but it was good enough. The coach wasn't leaving today, for sure.

Something occurred to her. "Higgins. May I have one moment?" she called after him.

He tilted his grey head the other way.

"I want to ask you something," she said loudly and slowly.

Higgins nodded.

"What happened to His Grace?" She pointed to her face.

"The face?"

"Yes."

"The war, Your Grace."

Of course.

"Waterloo?"

He nodded.

"How terrible."

Higgins shuffled away, muttering. "He's the only one who survived."

Birdie wondered whether he'd meant that metaphorically.

Either way, the man must have scars inside as well. No wonder he was rather antisocial.

"Higgins, what about dinner?" she called after him. She didn't want to have to spend a second evening in that frightful kitchen, cooking away on her own.

"There's haggis in the village," he mumbled.

"Don't we have a cook?"

Higgins shook his head.

"Who's been cooking all along?" Birdie pressed on. "You?"

Surprisingly, he'd understood her. He bared his yellowed teeth in a grin.

"We're going to have to do something about that," Birdie mumbled.

HE SHOULDN'T HAVE TOLD them to hold the right flank.

It was a logical decision. A decision made from his gut. Usually, his gut led him right. It had helped him survive.

He'd thought they could take cover in the orchard trees. They were camouflaged behind the foliage and shrubbery.

It had been a disastrous choice.

He should've sent them to the left.

He heard the gunshots again, the battery blast above his head; flames leapt, and chunks of mud, wood, and metal catapulted through the air. The smell of smoke, blood, and scorched flesh engulfed him.

He buried his head in his hands and gagged.

Left.

It should've been the left.

Amidst the smoke, a voice.

"Your Grace."

Smith, Blake, Brown, Merivale to the right.

Merivale. Merciful heavens! Merivale ...

Someone shook his arm.

"Your Grace. She won't leave."

He lowered his hands from his wet face. Higgins was in front of him. He was in his castle, not on the battlefield. He was safe.

"What?" His voice was rough.

"The girl. She won't leave."

Higgins. The odd man always showed up when one least needed him.

What did he say about the girl? The girl he'd married not three hours ago.

The girl who'd screamed in terror when she'd seen his face, ran, then returned and married him, only after she loudly professed that she would declare her vows if she could include the phrase "love", demanding in return that he "loved, obeyed and served" her as well. He'd said the vow.

A shudder ran through his body. It was as if that vow almost physically tied his fate to hers, to that girl who said he should call her Birdie, a name that oddly suited her. She tilted her head sideways when she looked at him like a bird.

He'd never met a stranger creature.

He'd carried her to the hall after she'd fainted. She hadn't been exactly a lightweight, for she had a full, womanly figure. But he'd carried heavier, stiffer bodies in the past. As she lay there, she'd looked frail and beautiful, and he'd carefully wrapped a plaid blanket around her as if she were a precious piece of porcelain.

She could be all too easy to love.

The sooner she left, the better.

And now Higgins was saying she wouldn't leave?

"What do you mean, she won't leave?" Gabriel asked.

"Been working again in the kitchen." Higgins scratched his head. "I thought it was the pixies who fried the sausages, but it was the girl. Now she's baking. Baking!" He sounded outraged.

Gabriel fingered a scar on his cheek thoughtfully. "She's supposed to take the carriage back to her home."

"Yes, yes, she's alone," Higgins muttered and left.

Dash it, the man had phases when he understood perfectly well, followed by episodes where he seemed entirely deaf and senile.

Gabriel hadn't had the heart to dismiss him. He'd been working for three dukes of Dunross. When Gabriel inherited the dukedom, Higgins had shown up at his doorstep in London and stuck to him with more persistence than mud stuck to his Hessians. He'd followed him here to Dunross castle. He'd become his shadow.

"I serve the Dukes of Dunross," he'd stubbornly repeated and refused to leave. He'd been half deaf back then already. Though sometimes Gabriel suspected the man was faking it and selectively choosing only what he wanted to hear.

Higgins was one thing. The bigger problem was: what on earth was he going to do if the girl refused to leave?

Why on earth would she want to stay? She had his name. She had a title. He'd guaranteed her financial support. He'd fulfilled his promise to her father. He had nothing else to offer. The castle was a dump of stone; there were no servants. The food was ghastly, and he himself looked like a veritable gargoyle. Even in the old days, when he'd apparently looked reasonably attractive, he never relished being out in town and about in society.

He'd been semi-relieved when his father asked him to marry his colleague's daughter. He wouldn't have to go courting.

He was a military man. He knew how to order a company around the battlefield. Or he had thought he did. He did not know what to do with ladies. He could hardly order her around like his soldiers, could he? He had no idea how to talk to a woman, least of all court one.

Especially one who had a sprinkle of fairy freckles on her nose and a quizzical glint in her hazel eyes, and who was now his wife.

He was thoroughly ruffled.

Her hands had been icy cold when he had placed her on the sofa. He'd looked down at her. A complete stranger. His wife. Yet he felt like he'd never carried a more precious bundle in his arms.

He shook himself. No, no, no, no. This wouldn't do. The girl had walked into his life a mere twenty-four hours ago, and he already worried about her.

He needed to get rid of her immediately, but didn't know how to go about doing that without forcefully carrying her into the carriage.

Suddenly, a tremendous crash reverberated through the castle.

He jumped.

By Jupiter. What was that?

Either the place was being invaded, or the girl was taking the castle apart.

Since he was relatively sure he'd helped defeat the French in battle five years ago, it must be the girl.

With a feeling of foreboding, he left his tower room.

CHAPTER 8

$\mathcal{B}$irdie was rearranging the furniture.

After all, she told herself, she was the Duchess of Dunross; this was her home, and she could bloody well do whatever she wanted. She was determined to make this place more homey. It needed a womanly touch. Since there were no servants to help her, she had to do things herself. But she was used to that.

Whenever Birdie decided to do something, she did so systematically and thoroughly. After Gabriel had fled—really, there was no other way to say it, he'd literally fled after she'd mentioned children—and Higgins had shuffled away, she'd been left alone in the gigantic medieval hall.

She had heard the carriage rumble into the courtyard and stop in front of the stairs. It was to take her home. She ignored it.

Her gaze now fell on the door to the right. It was a smaller, oaken door next to the fireplace that she'd not noticed before.

"Plan for the day: investigate the castle," she said aloud. She'd open each door, peek into each corner, discover every secret of this place. After all, this was to be her new home. A feeling of excitement overcame her.

The room behind the door was dark as the drapes were drawn. Birdie pulled them aside, releasing a shower of dust. She sneezed.

Weak daylight poured through the grimy windows.

Birdie turned and gasped.

This was a library. Heavy oaken bookshelves with gothic woodwork lined the walls. Thousands of books spilled out of the shelves in a disorderly fashion. Books were stacked on the ground, strewn on the table. She took a few steps and stumbled over a pile. It looked like someone had collected all the books in Scotland and crammed them into this room without any rhyme or reason. A portrait of a sour-looking man with a wig, eagle-like nose, and piercing eyes hung over the massive fireplace. The old duke, no doubt. Birdie pulled a face. Cobwebs hung from the ceiling, and a white veil of dust covered the books.

Birdie ran a finger over a shelf and inspected the thick layer of white powder on her finger. She sneezed.

"This needs some desperate cleaning," she mumbled. She bent down to pick up a pile of books when she noticed something strange. As dusty as this entire library was, one shelf to the right of the fireplace was clean and polished. A path cleared of books led right to it. But what was even odder was the arrangement of the bookshelves. Why were there additional bookshelves haphazardly set up in the middle of the room? It served neither a functional nor aesthetic purpose. If one were to move this shelf so it stood perpendicular to the adjacent wall, and get rid of the other one, which seemed to be placed at random and appeared half-empty, it would allow for more light in the room. And it wouldn't be so cluttered.

"Sometimes less is better," Birdie decided.

Birdie eyed the half-empty bookshelf. It should be easy to move. She took all the books out, set them on the floor, and gave it a push.

Her assessment had been correct, and she could, with some force, move the shelf right through the door into the hall.

She surveyed her work, satisfied. Maybe Higgins needed an additional bookshelf somewhere? One could move it to the kitchen to use for storing jars of preserved fruit.

Now, to the second shelf. Emboldened by her success, she gave the shelf a push. Except this one was heavier, and it still wouldn't move even after she had taken out the books. It moved an inch, then snagged on the carpet, which folded up and stopped any further movement.

Birdie pushed harder.

With a growl, she gave it a final push. The shelf wobbled and wobbled some more.

"Oh no. Oh, no, you don't!" Birdie tried to stem against it from the other side, but it had gathered momentum and crashed with tremendous force to the ground.

It sounded like an explosion.

The ground shook. The chandelier clanked.

Birdie clasped both hands over her ears and squeezed her eyes shut for good measure.

When she pried one eye open, she saw the entire library floor splattered with books. And the shelf had broken in half.

Running footsteps sounded in the hall.

"What the devil is going on?" a voice roared.

Gabriel's hair stuck in all directions, his dark eye flashed, and the side of his face that wasn't too handsome looked devastating when daylight shone directly on it. He truly looked like the Beast of Dunross castle.

She backed off involuntarily.

"I was rearranging the library." She lifted her chin. "It

needs to be cleaned. As does the rest of this place. And because there aren't any servants around here to do the job for me, I have to do it myself."

"Are you hurt?" he asked curtly, taking in the full disaster.

"No. I've somehow only received a small paper cut." She lifted a finger where a drop of blood oozed out. She popped it into her mouth.

"Why aren't you in the coach on the way home?" Gabriel asked with a sigh. "I thought I'd made it clear that you were to leave."

"And I thought I'd made it clear that I would be staying."

"Is it more money you want, then?"

"How dare you!" Birdie hissed at him. "Do you think I am the kind of person whom you can bribe by offering a sufficient amount of money?"

"Then why?"

Birdie picked up a book. "Why what?"

"Why are you still here?"

She glared at him in defiance. "Because I said a vow? I happen to take my vows very seriously, even if you don't."

She saw his shoulders slump. He pulled his hand through his hair. It was thick, wavy and dark brown—on one side. It was rather too long and in need of a haircut. Or he could bind it together as was fashionable in the previous century. And if he'd get a decent shave and get rid of that dark stubble and put on a neater set of clothes—even Birdie could tell what he was wearing was grossly out of fashion—he'd look devilishly handsome.

Gabriel pulled himself up and turned to her. In the light of day, she saw the thick red and blue welts crisscrossing the side of his face and down his neck. His skin appeared melted and welded together into thick lesions. His long, scraggly hair covered his ear. Birdie assumed it was partly gone. Not that it mattered, as the man seemed to hear very well without it.

"You are mistaken," Gabriel said hoarsely. "I take my vows very seriously. I made a vow to both our fathers before they died. I intend to fulfil it. But I can only do so successfully if you leave and carve out for yourself a life away from this unwholesome environment." He lifted a hand and waved around. She saw it was scarred as well. "Away from me." He added with a low voice. "There is no happiness to be had here. I can offer you my name and whatever money I have. But nothing more."

"Oh." Suddenly, Birdie understood. "I see. You think you will make me unhappy."

His shoulders drooped.

She picked up a pile of books from the floor and stacked them on the table. "What if I have decided that this––this rainy corner of Scotland––will suit me perfectly? This, admittedly, ghoulish place? And when you don't shout, growl, or snipe at me, you are not half bad to be around." She smiled.

Her husband looked taken aback.

"What on earth do you intend to do here? There is noth-ing––nothing at all for a young woman like you."

"Well, I wouldn't say that." Birdie set her hands against her hips. "I'd like to clean up this library, for one. I do like books, you know. Look!" She lifted a book. "A first Folio of Shakespeare! It's astounding!" She leafed through the book reverently and laughed out loud. "*The Taming of the Shrew*. Do you think this place has more treasures like this? Why aren't you taking better care of it?"

"I have no idea. And I couldn't care less." Gabriel shrugged. "This is the previous duke's home. He left it in shambles. The estates aren't any better." He threw up his hands in defeat. "Do what you need to do. I can't be bothered with any of it."

He turned and left abruptly.

Birdie stared after him with an open mouth. Had he just said he couldn't be bothered with it? With his own dukedom? What on earth?

Gabriel stopped in his tracks. "Also, thank you for those biscuits." He cleared his throat. "I haven't had biscuits since I was a child." Birdie had sent up Higgins with a plate of lavender biscuits earlier.

"Goodness me!" Birdie cried. "You poor man. How can one not eat biscuits for so long!"

He rubbed his neck. "One commonly isn't served lavender biscuits in the army."

"Of course not." Birdie decided immediately to bake up a storm. The poor man had to catch up.

She closed the book with a snap. After she was done with the house, she'd have to refurnish her husband.

CHAPTER 9

After having spent the entire day in the library, Birdie retreated to her room, tired and covered in dust. She'd never felt so dirty. There were still mud flecks in her clothes, and cobwebs in her hair. She'd tried to scrub the dirt off her face, neck and arms as best as could by dipping a towel into ice-cold water from the pitcher. She fervently wished for a hot bath. But who would carry the pails of hot water? Surely not Higgins.

She'd fallen into her large, canopied bed and slept like the dead. In the middle of the night, she sat straight up in bed, her heart hammering.

What was that?

Her hands grappled for the candle, and it took her three tries to light it.

She listened intently.

The castle seemed alive at night. There were unidentifiable sounds deep within its walls.

Footsteps. Thumps. Scraping, scratching sounds.

There were surely ghosts within these walls. Birdie shivered and drew her blanket closer around her.

"Stuff and nonsense, Roberta. There are no such things as ghosts." She padded the pillow around her head, lay down again and fell asleep.

BEFORE ANY KIND of refurbishing could happen to house, man, or otherwise, one needed to have man—or womanpower.

Which meant servants.

After Higgins had served another round of cold, lumpy porridge for breakfast, Birdie decided she had enough.

She pushed her spectacles up her nose and stared at the velvet purse that still lay on the table.

A plan formed in her mind.

The village. Maybe that was a place where she could get some more information.

And hire a cook.

And a maid.

And—she glanced about the room––a few girls to help clean out this place. It looked like the room hadn't been dusted since the Middle Ages.

She would begin her role as a duchess by visiting the cottages and delivering food baskets. For this is what duchesses commonly did. Birdie liked the idea excessively.

"I need baskets, Higgins," she told the butler as he cleared the table.

"A casket?"

"Bas-ket," she articulated. "You know. To put things in." She'd seen a collection of gooseberry jam jars on the shelves in the kitchen. The place certainly didn't lack in gooseberry jam, porridge and blood sausages. She could add a batch of sugar biscuits she'd quickly made this morning, in the presence of Higgins, who'd wrung his hands in agony the entire time. She'd given him a biscuit to munch on, and then he was quiet, and a blissful smile crossed his face. She'd given him three and a plate to take up to the duke. Ever since then, she had a niggling suspicion that she'd been elevated in Higgins' grudging respect. Suddenly, she could get anything she wanted. He'd even cleared the bookshelf away in the library —she wondered how he did it on his own. Maybe the man was stronger than he led on—and attempted some meagre dusting in the hall. Not that it had made much of a difference. She was still stuck with porridge for supper and that wouldn't do.

THE MORNING WAS blustery and cold as Birdie marched down the path to the village. Higgins, bless his soul, had obtained two small rickety baskets from a stable somewhere. She'd cleaned them as best as she could and filled them with the food she'd got from the larder.

"If only I could add something pretty, like flowers." But the only flowers she could see were purple thistles that grew along the stone wall. She picked several and adorned the basket with them. "It will have to do."

She hadn't seen Gabriel since their meeting in the library yesterday. She wondered what he did all day. What about his duties and obligations? So far, she hadn't seen him fulfilling any ducal duties at all.

The man was deeply wounded––and not just externally. But was that a reason to wall oneself up in this stone tower? He was a duke, not Rapunzel. Though, if he kept growing that hair, he could compete with Rapunzel for sure.

Soon, Birdie reached the quaint village and stopped outside a thatched hut. A group of children were playing in the muddy street. They stopped when she approached, looking at her curiously.

"Hello there. Are your mothers at home?" Birdie asked them.

A little urchin in bare feet, with mud on her face, stuck her thumb into her mouth and nodded.

"Where does she live, my dear?"

The girl pointed to another hut further down the dirt street.

Excellent.

Birdie rapped on the door in joyful anticipation of finally being able to execute her duty as a duchess.

The door opened, and a little boy stood in front of her. He had a shock of unruly red curls, tremendous eyes and was bare-footed. He had only one arm. The sleeve of his right arm was knotted together and dangled down at his side.

Birdie beamed at him. "Hello there. Who are you?"

"Tommy."

"Hello, Tommy. Is your mother here, perhaps?"

A woman came to the door and protectively planted her hands on the boy's shoulders.

"Good day. I'm Roberta Tal—I mean, I'm the new duchess. I married the duke yesterday. I wanted to introduce myself."

The woman narrowed her eyes. "Aye. They've read the banns in kirk the last three Sundays." The woman looked her up and down. She didn't look particularly friendly.

"And who might you be?" Birdie asked brightly.

"The name's McKenna."

"Mrs McKenna. I have a basket for you, something small, nothing special—" Birdie handed her the basket. The woman took it reluctantly.

"I didna expect—" She interrupted herself. Evidently, Birdie didn't fulfil her expectation of what a duchess should look like. The woman looked down at the basket.

"I hope you like this. I apologise for the selection. I made the biscuits myself. I thought, maybe the children would like them."

A look of surprise crossed the woman's face. "Ye made these yersel?"

"Yes. I rather enjoy baking."

"Ye bake these yersel?" she repeated. Birdie nodded. The woman took a biscuit out and bit into it. "It's... good." The note of surprise in her voice grew.

"I whiled away much of my time in the kitchen where I grew up. Sometimes I helped Cook cut out biscuits. I like to add some lavender to them. It gives them this extra special taste..." Her voice petered out as she took in the woman's abode.

It was dark and dank inside. Aside from a straw pallet where a bulky figure lay, the room had only a rickety table with two chairs and a shelf with pots. She'd never seen such poverty. Birdie tore her gaze away and smiled at the woman.

"I'm Eilidh McKenna," the woman snapped.

"Eilidh. What a pretty name. Are these your children?" Birdie turned to the three urchins that had crowded around them, curiously looking at her. She gave them some biscuits, which they took shyly.

"Aye."

"Eilidh, I was wondering if you could be of assistance to me. The castle is sadly understaffed. Do you know where I can find people who might be willing to help out?"

Eilidh's eyes grew. She looked away. "No. Naebody would work... up there."

"Eilidh!" a rough voice sounded from inside. It seemed to belong to the bulky figure lying on the bed. "Who is this?"

The figure rose from the bed and walked towards them. He was a rough-looking man.

"My husband," Eilidh explained. "Logan, this is the new

duchess. She's brought us a basket." Logan was tall and would have been a good-looking fellow if he groomed himself better. His auburn hair stuck out in all directions. His beard was matted and tangled. His eyes were bloodshot, and he reeked of alcohol. Birdie took an involuntary step back.

"We don't need no basket. We don't need no duchess neither," Logan snapped.

His wife pulled him back into the house. "Oh, whisht. This is for the bairns. And look, a bottle of wine." Logan took the bottle, uncorked it and sniffed at it. He shot Birdie a mistrustful look.

"As I was telling your wife, I am looking for people to hire," Birdie said nervously as she fiddled with her shawl.

"Nae."

"But why?"

"I forbid it."

"Excuse me, Mr McKenna, but it's not up to you whether I hire people in the castle or not."

He shrugged.

"I happen to need a maid," Birdie continued. "A housekeeper. And a cook. And two, or three, or more people who clean up the place. You would be paid, of course."

Eilidh's head snapped up. "Paid?"

"Of course. Make no mistake, his Grace will pay any retainers he hires. He won't be ungenerous. Well, I have to go. If you know anyone who might be interested in work, be sure to let me know."

Birdie hesitated. For a moment, she hoped Eilidh would speak. But no, Eilidh shot a fearful look at her husband, who was drinking directly out of the bottle of wine.

"Nae is nae, and that is nae," he said and burped.

Eilidh shook her head and closed the door.

Birdie sighed and turned to go.

She delivered the second basket to the reverend's wife,

who was grateful to receive it. There, too, she asked whether she could help with finding domestics. Mrs McAloy was more talkative than Eilidh.

"That will be a challenge, Your Grace. The old duke was none too popular. And the new one..." Her voice petered away. "People are afraid. Which is nonsense, of course. My husband says he's a perfectly normal man. Despite his—you know." She gestured with her hand to one side of her face. "He's a recluse, though, and that doesn't help. The people look on him with mistrust."

Birdie nodded. "What about the old duke? What was wrong with him?"

Mrs McAloy's face darkened. "He was an evil man. Bled the people, and the land, dry. He let the estate degenerate and now it is as you see it. The people here are poor. They have no fondness for neither old nor new duke." Her face softened as she looked upon Birdie. "But you seem to be a sensible young woman, Your Grace. Forgive me for speaking familiarly, but you remind me of my daughter. It is kind of you to have delivered the baskets. The people here receive little kindness. God bless."

Birdie pondered on Mrs McAloy's words on her way back to the castle. She took a small, pebbled side-path that wound itself up the mount where the castle perched. Turning around, she saw the village nestled underneath. On the other side, the ocean stretched in front of her, calm and blue. She inhaled a big breath of fresh salt air. Life wouldn't be too bad here, if they'd give her a chance to settle.

She heard quick footsteps and laboured breathing behind her. Birdie whirled around. It was Eilidh.

"Your Grace." Eilidh reached her and halted, panting. Her eyes flitted back furtively to check if someone was there. Then she continued, "My sister can do it. Be yer maid. She's worked fer a lady fer seven years. She's clean. Can take care of a lady's wardrobe, do her hair and all else. And I can sew. I used to be a seamstress before I married Logan, and he brought me here. I also ken someone who cooks real well. And I know some girls who'd love to earn a penny or two cleaning."

"Eilidh, that is wonderful." Birdie clasped Eilidh's rough hands between hers.

"The problem is, miss, I mean, Yer Grace, that the men cannae know. Especially mine."

"Well, that's bound to be a problem. Whyever not?" Birdie frowned. They desperately needed money, yet they wouldn't let the women work. How so?

Eilidh shook her head. "That's the condition on which we can work. We can do it fer a certain time only during the day while they're out at sea. An' we've got bairns."

Birdie nodded slowly. "The village school?"

"Nae teacher. The school master's left after a tiff a year ago because no one could pay him."

Birdie patted the woman's rough hands.

"Don't you worry about the children. I'll make sure they'll be taken care of. Bring whoever is willing to work tomorrow morning."

"Yes ma'am. Yer Grace." The woman bobbed her head, bowed, and ran back down the hill.

Birdie's brain set in motion. She returned to the castle feeling that she had accomplished something that day.

CHAPTER 10

"Your Grace, we're being invaded!" Higgins, who never rushed, ran, or spoke loudly, managed to do all three, startling Gabriel so that he dropped the figure he was holding in his hand.

"Whatever is the matter, Higgins?" his master asked.

"Women!" The man leaned a hand against the wall as he gasped. "The castle is invaded by women."

Higgins must be delusional. Maybe it had been too much for him to take care of the girl, but how one girl could multiply into many was beyond him. Gabriel watched with concern as Higgins wheezed and gasped for breath.

"You shouldn't be running. Not even during an invasion." Gabriel picked up the figure he'd been painting and set it down on his table.

Higgins gestured with his hand to the door. "I've never experienced anything like it. Come and see for yourself."

Gabriel crept stealthily down the corridor as if approaching an unsuspecting enemy.

Indeed, there were noises in the main hall that sounded

suspiciously like a gaggle of women. Was his wife holding a tea party?

He stopped on the top stairs, went down to his knees, from there lay on his stomach and peeked between the wooden bars of the baluster. It was in the same manner he'd lain in the ridge near Hougoumont and observed Napoleon's troops approach. From this point, he could gather intelligence without being seen.

Except these weren't Napoleon's troops. It was something worse. They were women, indeed.

One of them was his wife. She was eagerly talking, gesticulating with her hands as she appeared to be directions to a group of women who held mops, buckets and brooms. Then they spread in all directions to their assigned places.

Heaven help him.

They were going to clean the place!

Higgins was entirely right. It was an invasion of the grossest sort.

He felt oddly helpless. She really was determined to settle down here, was she? She was going to clean up this place. Other than firmly locking his door and staying out of sight, there was nothing he could do about it unless he revealed himself.

Face a group of women?

He broke out in a sweat.

He'd rather face Boney's firing squad.

He crept back to his room, feeling defeated.

IT HAD BEEN A SATISFYING DAY.

For the first time in a fortnight, Birdie finally had her bath.

She also had a maid, Ally, who helped her. She whispered

when she talked, so Birdiehad to tell her to speak up several times. Ally was a shy girl who'd worked previously as a maid in a manor house near Edinburgh. When the lady of the house passed away, she was dismissed from her post, and she had travelled north to live with her sister and her family. She worked quietly, flitting from room to room like a shadow. She pressed, folded, and put away Birdie's clothes, and mended tears and holes in her stockings. She also tamed Birdie's unruly hair, deftly tying it into a bun that did not look too severe, teasing out some locks that stayed in shape.

Birdie now had a pretty new dress that Eilidh, with her nimble fingers, had quickly produced. Eilidh had spoken the truth when she'd said she knew how to sew. Birdie's wardrobe was full of old dresses that were long out of fashion. Eilidh promised she would take them one by one and adjust them for her. That woman could sew a ball gown out of the dusty curtains without blinking if she told her to.

Birdie stroked the dark blue velvet material of her new dress. It was warm, and it matched the plaid shawl. She thought it looked good on her.

The new cook, Mrs Gowan, made traditional Scottish food. For supper tonight they'd have Cullen Skink, she'd announced. It turned out to be a creamy soup with smoked haddock, potatoes, onions, served with toasted bread. Birdie had never eaten anything so divine. Well, after her diet of porridge and sausage, anything would taste divine.

The duke, however, hadn't come down for supper. He'd been notoriously absent the entire day. Birdie wondered what he was doing.

LATER, she wandered into a room that must've been a study. It had mahogany shelves crammed with books. An oak writing table stood in the middle of the room. She assumed it was the old duke's study, long since abandoned.

Birdie went to the table and opened the drawers. They were stuffed with papers, books, bills.

Sitting in the heavy leather chair, she emptied the drawers.

At the bottom were two leather books.

Ledgers. She flipped one open and studied the numbers. "Whoever did the accounting here must have had a horrid sense of numbers," she said as she shook her head. Then she grabbed a quill and calculated.

After two hours, she rubbed her eyes. The candles were burning low. Was there any point in trying to decipher the ledgers further? She could make neither head nor tail of it. Either someone had badly tampered with the numbers, or she was simply too tired to calculate.

She tucked the ledgers under her arm and wandered into the drawing room, which looked quite comfortable now that the holland covers had been removed. The room had been cleaned, the carpets beaten, and the curtains and windows washed. It was a wood-panelled room with a threadbare old sofa and a pianoforte. She had taken little notice of the instrument before but now had a desire to try it out.

Birdie sat down on the stool and pressed a key. The piano was badly out of tune.

Regardless, she played a simple Mozart melody that she'd been taught at the seminary. Birdie was an indifferent player. She would never be as accomplished as her friend Arabella, who played piano to an almost professional level. She was out of practice and did not have the music sheets to help her along.

Sensing a presence behind her, she paused, her hands hovering above the keys.

"That was atrocious," a voice behind her said.

She whirled around. Gabriel was leaning against the doorway, his arms crossed. A lock of black hair fell across his face, shadowing his injured side. He was in shirtsleeves, his shirt tucked in one side of his breeches and hanging loose on the other. He looked handsome, dangerous, wild.

Birdie's pulse increased, and suddenly the room seemed too small.

"I thought I was doing rather well. Not a single mistake." She hammered down on the keys again.

Gabriel winced.

"It's the piano. It's out of tune," Birdie explained as she played another chord.

"You're hacking onto the keys with brute force. You have to play with more feeling."

"Oh?" She hammered down once more. "I think it sounds rather good."

Gabriel hovered by the doorway, hesitating as if he couldn't decide whether he wanted to enter or leave. Birdie wondered what had brought him out of his den. Was it really the atrociousness of her playing?

"I found something in the desk's drawer." Birdie got up. She picked up the ledgers and handed them to him. "You should look at them. There is something deeply wrong with those numbers, but I can't figure out what it is."

He didn't take them.

"Don't you want to have a look at them?"

"It is no concern of mine."

Birdie almost dropped the books. "What! This is about your estate! Your lands, your tenants, your income. Normally, dukes have a steward who takes care of it. But since you aren't possessed of even the most basic of serving staff, maybe it is to be expected that you do not have a steward, either."

He tucked his hands under his armpits. "You brought in all those women today. What did you think you were doing?"

She thought that was obvious. Lifting a hand, she waved it about as if to show him the room in all its glory. "They were cleaning the castle. It was well overdue. Don't you like what they did today? This castle is actually not that bad when you've cleared away all the muck and grime."

"I preferred it the way it was before."

Birdie stared at him. "I am about to throw the candlestick at you," she declared, reaching for the candlestick.

Gabriel ducked immediately. He looked so ridiculously alarmed that an involuntary laugh escaped her, which took the gravity out of the situation.

"I take it you paid them from the pouch I gave you," her husband asked.

Birdie thought of how that pouch was now considerably lighter than it was before. She shrugged.

He scowled. "The money was meant to be for you, not for paying servants."

Birdie folded her arms. "Someone has to pay the servants."

"How often do I have to say it: I don't need anyone other than Higgins." Gabriel jutted out his chin like a spoilt child.

Dear me. The man was dumb, deaf, or inordinately stubborn. But then, so was she. Well, just stubborn. She was definitely not dumb, and certainly not deaf. She peeked at the man before her. Why did she have the impression he was sulking? Could he seriously be miffed because she told someone to mop the floor?

"We also have a cook now who is capable of cooking more than porridge," she chattered on. "Higgins will no longer have to spend his valuable time in the kitchen but will be able to devote himself to more important things. Where is he anyhow?"

"He left. He leaves every night."

"What? Where to?"

Gabriel shrugged. "He has a room in one of the outer houses."

"You are saying that he doesn't sleep in the castle?"

"It would seem so."

"But why?"

"It appears he is afraid of ghosts. Along with the rest of them."

Birdie digested his words. The women had left at dusk. As far as she knew, not because they were afraid of ghosts, but because they needed to be home before the men returned from work. That was a slightly different matter. Tomorrow morning, they would return.

"Are you saying that all this time, you spent your nights all alone in the castle?" Birdie could hardly believe it.

Gabriel shrugged and turned to go. She followed him, breathless.

"Wait. Can you just tell me one thing?"

He stopped in his tracks.

"Just so I understand. Why do you want to live in the midst of,"––she waved her hand––"ruin, decay and dirt?" She refused to believe he enjoyed it. "Why not make it a home?"

"This isn't my home. It never will be." He turned around suddenly, looking straight into her eyes. His were a deep, dark chocolate brown. And deeply sad. "And it will never be your home, either."

He stopped in front of a massive door that led up the tower stairs. He opened it with a key.

"Where are you going?" Birdie eyed the heavy door, remembering the first night in the castle when she'd fled in fright after having seen him for the first time. Her cheeks heated in embarrassment.

"To my room. Alone," Gabriel said without turning around and slammed the door in her face. She heard his footsteps on the stone stairs winding up the tower.

Birdie sighed and left, knowing that, except for her husband in the tower, she was all alone in the castle.

THAT NIGHT she heard it again. The scratching and scraping. The footsteps. She shivered in her bed, wrapped herself even more tightly in her blanket and told herself there was no such thing as ghosts. It was Gabriel, walking up and down in his room. Maybe he couldn't sleep, either. Or perhaps Higgins doing whatever butlers usually did. But Higgins wasn't in the castle. And it was nearly midnight.

At around half past midnight, she sat up.

"Roberta Talbot, you are a goose." She pulled on a second dress, thick stockings and a coat. Taking a candle and a lantern, she went on a ghost hunt.

CHAPTER 11

*T*here are ghosts and then there are ghosts, her friend Lucy used to tell them at the seminary.

During one particularly eery night, the girls huddled around her in their local graveyard with nothing but a single candle burning in a lamp.

"Most ghosts," Lucy explained, "are not really ghosts at all. They're but figments of the imagination. Real ghosts are not visible to the rational eye. A draft of cold air. A feeling of apprehension. Goosebumps covering the arm. This is how genuine ghosts make themselves known. They're mostly harmless."

"But Lucy. What about poltergeists, creatures who throw down porcelain cups and knock on doors?" Arabella asked. "Apparently, we have several of those at Ashmore Hall."

"Pooh. I will tell you a secret. Come closer." The girls huddled closer.

"The secret," Lucy whispered, her low voice hollow, caused Birdie to shiver in anticipation. "The secret is"--she paused dramatically as the whites of her eyes glittered--

"that there are no such things as poltergeists! Whoo hoo!" With a howl, she pulled out a white sheet and threw it into the air. It fluttered in the night wind, like a spectre. The girls screamed. The sheet fluttered to the ground and looked, well, like a sheet. Huddling closer, the girls clung to each other and burst into laughter.

"You're terrible, Lucy. Giving us such a fright!" Birdie's heart hammered against her chest, but she laughed.

"Oh pooh. Keep this in mind. If you ever try to impersonate a ghost, remain normal. Ghosts used to be people with personalities once upon a time. No white linen sheets, for pity's sake! Lest you encounter the same fate as poor Thomas Millwood. He was mistaken for the Hammersmith Ghost and shot."

"The Hammersmith Ghost? Oh my. What happened?" Birdie asked as she clasped the hands in front of her breast.

"Poor Thomas Millwood was wearing white linen work clothes that fluttered in the wind. He was a plasterer. He crossed the graveyard when an officer mistook him for the Hammersmith ghost." Lucy shrugged. "Rather stupid of the officer, I must add. Thinking he could shoot a ghost!"

The girls looked around nervously, glad they were wearing dark coats.

"Mind you, it's the frightful atmosphere of the graveyard that plays on your imagination. Not this old sheet on the ground." Lucy nudged it with her foot. "If I'd done this in plain daylight, you wouldn't have blinked an eyelash. Remember this: things never are what they appear to be."

Lucy pulled out a book and read them a wonderfully spooky tale. It had been one of the scariest and most delightful outings during her time at school.

Birdie grinned in fond memory as she trudged down the dark hall of the castle.

Having been previously initiated in the lore of ghosts, in a cemetery no less, she felt more than ready to confront the Ghost of Dunross Castle.

Moonlight flooded through the gothic windows, casting long shadows. Her lamp illuminated little of the hall, but there was sufficient light for her to see that there was not a soul there.

So far, this was not surprising. Then, she frowned. There were odd sounds; grating sounds that seemed like they came from the library. She went in there. Throwing the door open, it did not surprise her that the room was empty.

She let her eyes roam. The only ghostly thing in the room was the portrait of the old duke, whose pale face and malevolent eyes glared down on her. Birdie shuddered. She would tell Higgins to take down this portrait first thing in the morning. There was nothing else here. Turning toward the door, Birdie's gaze fell on the window. She froze.

What on earth was that?

She almost dropped her lamp. She squinted through the window. Why hadn't she brought her spectacles? There was something outside on the far end of the bailey, on the battlement. She blinked in surprise. Indeed.

It was a ghost.

A white thing that fluttered in the air, ghostlike and terrifying. It looked exactly like Lucy's sheet. Except this one had two red, glowing eyes.

Birdie tilted her head sideways.

Red glowing eyes? Somehow, that didn't fit in with anything Lucy had told her about ghosts.

"We will see about that," Birdie muttered. She went to the front door and rattled on the latch.

That Higgins. She would have to tell him to stop locking them into the castle. He simply would also have to sleep in the castle, like any other proper butler.

Birdie kicked the heavy door, frustrated. It merely made a

dull thump; the door remained firmly shut, and her toe smarted.

This just wouldn't do.

BIRDIE ROSE EARLY the next morning and went down to the front hall. She found the door unlocked. She crossed the bailey and took the stone steps up the battlements that surrounded the castle. There, she found exactly what she expected to find.

A piece of wire and a wrinkled sheet with eye holes hidden in the parapet's recess. Next to it was a pot with dirt, a broom, and a lamp with coals.

Clever.

Someone had stuck the broom into the dirt pot and used wire to fix a sheet on it. Underneath, he or she had placed a lamp with glowing coals. On top of the gloomy castle battlements in the middle of the night, anyone with the faintest belief in the supernatural would think this was a ghost.

She thought about packing the "ghost" up and taking it with her, but changed her mind and put it back into the stone recess. No need to alarm whoever deemed it necessary to come up with this ridiculous ploy.

Someone had gone through some considerable trouble to put a fright into her.

The question was: who?

And why? Someone who wanted her gone.

Higgins? Gabriel?

It made little sense. Higgins had nothing to gain by scaring her. And Gabriel? After having married her, he'd moved heaven and hell to get rid of her. Would that include frightening her away? Why would he go to such measures?

Huffing, she stomped down the stairs of the battlement. Her husband had some explaining to do.

CHAPTER 12

*B*irdie found the door to the tower unlocked. She opened it with determination and went up the winding staircase. Her husband really lived in Rapunzel's tower, completely isolated from the rest of the world.

Fully expecting the door to the room to be locked, she pressed down on the handle and to her surprise, found that the door opened without as much as a creak. It occurred to her too late that she should've knocked.

She cleared her throat and knocked on the door frame. "Uh. Is anyone here?" she called out.

No answer.

She pushed the door open and found herself once more inside the round tower room. It was gothic, medieval, from another time and age. The first night she'd been here, she'd seen only the fireplace and the armchair.

Speechless, she looked about. There was a small window, as was customary for tower rooms. It allowed sufficient light. A small fireplace was on the other side. A simple bed, more of a cot. Was this where he slept? With nothing but a thin woollen blanket and a lumpy straw pallet?

Like a soldier.

Birdie stroked her hand over the blanket. It was rough and thin.

What kind of man was her husband? Why did he voluntarily wall himself up in this room to live in dirt and poverty? Why marry her and then tell her to leave? Did he have anything to do with that ghost yesterday?

He was a mystery, her husband.

There were some books stacked by the bed. But what caught her attention was what stood in the middle of the room. On a low platform supported by books, taking up the entire room was a model of some sort. Plates of paint and brushes were scattered on the floor.

Birdie stepped up to it, careful not to step on the paint. Amazed, she saw that it was a landscape. There were hills, fields, and a forest. Crafted out of clay and papier mâché and meticulously painted. There were hundreds of miniature figures everywhere. She picked up one.

Tin soldiers? Armies of them. Some in red, some blue, green, blue-white...

Then she understood. She was looking at a battle scene.

These troops over there must be the French. She picked up a figure that resembled the Emperor of the French: Napoleon on a white steed.

And this one here, a figure on a brown horse with a bicorn hat and a simple blue coat with gilt buttons. Wellington. Birdie marvelled at how detailed the figure was. Every tiny button, every crease of the coat was wonderfully painted. Birdie set it back carefully.

Another figure stood out. It wore a scarlet red coat with a white cross belt and grey trousers. It lay behind a farm with blackened, collapsed walls. The face was half blackened. Birdie gasped.

She picked up the figure and walked over to the window

to see it better. On the windowsill, on a black velvet cloth, was a pistol. Ready and loaded.

She picked it up with trembling fingers.

"What are you doing?" a voice roared behind her. She dropped the figure and nearly the pistol as well.

"I am so sorry. I just—I didn't—I didn't mean—" She set the pistol down carefully.

"This is private," Gabriel snarled. "Haven't you wrought enough havoc in the rest of the castle? Must you also invade my private quarters?"

He stalked towards her with a scowl.

Birdie took a step backwards, stumbled over a pile of books and sprawled on the floor.

"You are a plague upon man. Get out. Get out now and never come back!" Her husband picked up a book. His face had turned completely red; a vein pulsated in his temple, and his one remaining eye flashed.

Birdie picked herself up, tumbled out of the door and down the stairs.

She heard him slam the door behind her, followed by a vicious thump against the door.

He'd thrown a book against it.

TEARS RAN down her face as she stumbled down the stairs.

He was insane.

He'd lost his mind completely.

Not only was he caught up in the past, but he was also suicidal. Birdie choked. He was going to kill himself the moment she left. That had been the plan all along. What was it with the men in her life who, rather than taking a chance on her, loving her, preferred to kill themselves?

Like her father. He'd also had a pistol, and he'd used it.

Even her brother Freddie had tried in a duel, but he'd failed.

She ran out the door and across the bridge. As she ran down the path to the village, her skirt tangled up with the nettles on the way. She pulled it loose.

Her hammering heart slowed down gradually.

All she wanted was a chance.

A chance at what?

Love?

Birdie laughed harshly and rubbed her cheeks with her hand.

Of course, she couldn't expect him to love her, vow or not. After all, they'd just met several days ago. But she was at least willing to make it work. Even if it was just friendship, or if that was too much to ask, basic kindness and courtesy toward one another. Why was that too much to ask? Life was too lonely otherwise. Too harsh. Too unbearable.

Fat tears rolled down her cheeks again.

She couldn't force people to like her. She couldn't force *him* to accept her. Maybe the better option was to leave and let him do what he needed to do.

But what would she do?

Where could she go?

She'd long lost her position at the Willowburys. Perhaps Cecily had assumed her identity and taken her job under her name.

She could return to her family. Chances were that they'd never even noticed she was gone. Her mother would lie on her bed the entire day, in a darkened room, and her sisters would pretend to get ready for balls that never happened. Freddie would be out gambling and return drunk––if he returned at all.

She used to like her brother, once. He'd been a cheerful boy who always got into scrapes. He listened with glistening eyes and an open mouth whenever she read to him. But that was before he turned into a dandy, discovered gambling and alcohol, and adopted the ennui of the world-weary. She hadn't had a proper conversation with him in years.

A cold stone settled in her stomach.

She knew she wouldn't be able to stand it there for long. Sooner or later they would need money. They always needed money. And Birdie would set out and obtain it for them. Because she was the only one who could.

She wiped her cheek angrily.

There was the allowance, of course. But she refused to take a penny from Gabriel. She would have no part in his plan. She would never forgive herself if she did.

She could go to Lucy or to Arabella in Cornwall. But both had their own families. While she knew they'd welcome her with open arms, she couldn't stay longer than a month or two. And then what? Surely they could help her find a position somewhere. As a companion. But they would probably never allow that and insist she stay with them.

She'd feel like a charity case, living with them.

It was unbearable. Unbearable!

Pondering her options, Birdie realised she didn't have any choices at all. Why was life so limiting for women? Why couldn't she choose a profession like a man? She knew she would be so good at so many things. If she could, she would've gone to university. Studied Law, maybe. Medicine. She'd always been an excellent student and enjoyed learning. But that path was not available to women.

Birdie shivered. A cold gust came from the sea, and she trembled further; she'd forgotten to put on her coat. She'd trudged down a small path through the meadow that led to the cliffs. She paused under an apple tree and looked around. Was this once an apple orchard? It needed to be tended to.

Another one of those things that would never get done because the lord of the estate did not care.

"Yer Grace, Yer Grace!" a voice called after her. Eilidh came hurrying after her.

"Eilidh." Birdie smiled weakly. Eilidh had done wonderful work refashioning the old gowns for Birdie. But she wasn't up to talking to her now.

"I've been wantin' to ask. About school." Eilidh breathed heavily.

"School?" Birdie looked at her blankly.

"Ye ken. For the bairns."

"Oh! Yes. I did mention that." Birdie sighed. She'd been too hasty, making promises she couldn't keep.

"I've been thinking. If ye didn't mind. More of us would come to work up there if we had our bairns taken care of at school. I was meanin' to ask Her Graceship if ye could teach them?"

Birdie stared at her, not at all comprehending. "Are you asking whether I could teach the children?"

The woman nodded eagerly.

"But that's entirely out of the question." Birdie shook her head. "I cannot teach. And even if I could. It's not possible. I am leaving," she blurted out.

Eilidh's stricken eyes flew to her face. "Leavin'? But why?"

"It was a mistake to come here. I never should've to begin with." It was the truth, wasn't it?

Eilidh shook her head. "But ye just married the duke. Ye cannae just leave."

Birdie slumped against the tree. "I'm afraid this kind of arrangement is common for people in our class. Dukes marry, and then they send their wives away to lead separate lives."

"And ye will go along with this nonsense?" Eilidh crossed her arms.

"Why stay where you're not wanted?" The bitterness in Birdie's voice surprised even her. The moistness in her eyes was just the wind, she told herself.

Eilidh scrutinised her face. Her features softened. "Yer Grace. I beg yer pardon. But I must ask."

Birdie scrubbed a hand over her eyes wearily. "What, Eilidh?"

"Do ye love him?"

There it was again. Love. "No! Of course I don't... love him."

They didn't even know each other. The couple of times they'd met, she'd run away screaming, or he'd thrown a book after her.

Yet she'd spoken vows of love not three days ago. A chill swept through Birdie. She'd not only lied; she'd said a vow she never meant, the gravity of which she did not truly comprehend.

Birdie felt utterly wretched. "I'm a terrible person, Eilidh," she whispered.

"Nay, ye aren't. Ye're confused." Eilidh shook her head. "It's the men. Always the men. We do everything we can for them. Feed them. Clean them. Keep their house. Give them bairns. And what do we get in return? A beating, that's what."

"Eilidh! Your husband isn't beating you?"

"Yer fate is yer fate, and mine is mine. I used to love him, once. Did not see what kind he truly was." She shrugged. "Now it's too late."

"Why don't you leave him?"

Eilidh looked at Birdie as if she had two heads. "How can you ask? The bairns, of course."

"Of course," Birdie echoed.

"Everything I do is for my bairns. And what they need the most right now is a school. Stay, and teach the children, Yer Grace. I ask this of ye as a mother."

Teach the children.

She'd run away from teaching children. Now she should do so voluntarily?

It was certainly an assignment. Rather different from teaching spoiled offspring of noblemen. These children would need to be taught everything from the basics. It would be more elemental. More real.

They needed her.

It would have a purpose.

It would do them all good.

"I will think about it, Eilidh." Birdie said slowly.

Eilidh took Birdie's hand between her two rough ones. "God bless ye, Yer Grace."

BIRDIE RETURNED TO THE CASTLE, deep in thought. She'd as good as promised Eilidh to set up a village school. She couldn't simply leave without doing at least that for them. If something good could come out of this entire situation, maybe this was it. Yes. She'd do this. Set up a school. Make sure the children were taken care of. Then she could leave with good conscience.

Setting up a school, of course, wasn't done just like that. One needed so many things …

Birdie's mind whirled as she made a mental list of all the items she'd need.

She stood in the middle of her room, back to the door as she pulled her dress over her head. A timid knock sounded at the door.

That must be Ally. The girl was a blessing to have about. She was quiet, courteous, and seemed to enjoy being Birdie's maid. Not like that quarrelsome Mary who pulled her mouth into a sour line when she helped pull up Birdie's stockings.

"Come in," Birdie said as she struggled into her gown.

"Help me button up, please. I can't reach the top buttons in the back."

It took her rather long to button her up, Birdie thought. Once or twice, Ally's fingers brushed her nape as if in a gentle caress. She felt the little, fine hairs on her arms rise. With a half-laugh, Birdie tilted her head sideways to brush her fingers off.

"Thank you, Ally." She turned around, and an involuntary scream tore out of her throat. For this wasn't Ally.

Gabriel lifted his hands as if to ward off her scream. "Please. No more screaming. I daresay your scream terrifies me more than my unfortunate visage frightens you." He'd backed off so far that his back almost touched the wall. "Though you are not to blame, of course. Not in the least."

Birdie snapped her mouth shut. "Goodness me." She pressed her hand against her chest. He was in shirtsleeves and wore beige coloured breeches that looked like they came from the previous century. He looked like a pirate through and through. Birdie's heart hammered, but she was certain that it was no longer from surprise.

Gabriel rubbed the scar on his cheek. "I seem to have the unfortunate habit of giving you a fright. I came to—to—apologise." He stepped from one foot to another. "My behaviour earlier was inexcusable. It was ungentlemanly and entirely unacceptable. I don't usually shout at women." He took a big breath. "I usually don't shout at all. Except at my men. When the French attack. To keep them from dying. My men. Not the French. They were meant to die." No doubt it dawned on him that he was bungling his apology horribly. He closed his eyes, swallowed, and tried again. "My only weak excuse is that you took me by surprise. But even that is no excuse for my behaviour. I have no words. Pray accept my apology." He awkwardly gestured to a small bundle of flowers that he'd placed on the table before he'd buttoned up her dress.

Birdie picked up the little flower bundle. It was a simple bouquet of purple bell heather. Had he truly scrambled about the moors to pick the flowers for her?

As if reading her thoughts, a red blush crept over his cheeks. "They grow everywhere on the hills behind the castle. I see them from my window. The entire field is purple with those things."

She looked at him sternly. "Did you ask Higgins to pick them?"

He cleared his throat and mumbled something.

Birdie bent forward. "I did not understand."

He cleared his throat again. "I said, I went out and picked them myself." His face was most definitely glowing red.

Birdie stared into his face. "You actually left your hermit's tower to pick flowers for me."

He rubbed his neck. "Er, yes."

"When was the last time you were outside in the fresh air?" Birdie took a cup, poured water in it from a pitcher and arranged the flowers in it.

"It's been a while." He cleared his throat. "It may have been the first time since I arrived at the castle. No, that's not correct. Our, er, wedding day. I walked through the bailey, twice."

Birdie gaped. "Aside from that, you never left the castle the entire time since your arrival?"

He lifted one shoulder.

"For how long?"

He didn't reply.

Birdie pushed up her spectacles and glared at him. "How long?"

"It may have been two years," he mumbled. "Or three."

She shook her head, horrified. "No wonder you're as white as a ghost." She placed her hands on her hips. "You have to go out more often. The fresh air and sun will be good for you."

He looked at her curiously. "Yes, ma'am." Then he laughed. "The last time someone scolded me like this, it may well have been my mother."

"As any good mother would! Three years of voluntary imprisonment." Birdie clasped her hands together. "It is inconceivable. And before that?"

"I was in London. I barely recall. Higgins found me and brought me here."

"Well, thank goodness for Higgins. And before London?" She was determined to squeeze his entire life story out of him.

He shrugged. "The Peninsular War and all that."

"Right. So the model in your room was a war scene? It was incredible! All that detail! I've never seen the likes of it."

His face shut down. "Yes. I am trying to reconstruct it."

"May I ask why?"

At first, he looked like he would not answer. "To get it out of my mind," he gritted through his teeth. Then he turned on his heels. "I won't disturb you any longer."

"Wait." Birdie racked her brain. "How old are you?" she blurted out. It was the first thing that had come to her mind.

Gabriel turned an even darker shade of red. "Thirty-five," he muttered. "Old enough to know that a gentleman does not shout at ladies."

She took a big breath. "You have not, by any chance, ever seen a ghost here, have you? Or maybe even impersonated a ghost?"

"Impersonate a ghost?" He looked so comically flabbergasted that Birdie almost laughed. "Why would I do that?"

"To keep intruders at bay. With white sheets and such."

He shook his head, then pulled a face. "You have given me

an idea, there. Maybe I should try this to keep people away from me."

"Are people so terrible to have about?"

He shrugged.

She played with the petals of the bouquet. "I know you don't want me here. But I still don't understand why you'd marry a girl, only to send her away an hour later."

Gabriel opened and closed his mouth. Birdie continued before she lost the momentum: "I am particularly angry because you haven't even attempted to get to know me. You haven't given us a chance."

"Us?" His voice sounded hoarse.

"Yes. You won't even consider it. I would like to ask this of you: I will leave, if that is what you want, but give me a month to prove you wrong. Give our marriage a chance."

There was a long pause. Then Gabriel said, "I don't know whether that would be wise."

More stubborn than a donkey. She decided to change tactics. "Then give me a chance to do something for the villagers here. They need my help. They need your help."

His face shut down. "I do not intend to get involved in the locals' lives."

"But you're a duke!" Birdie threw up her hands. "You have duties! You have estates! The people depend on you! Don't you care at all about their welfare? Think about all the good you can do?"

"This, madam, is where I beg to disagree."

"In other words, you refuse to take responsibility for them."

"So it would seem." His voice had turned frosty.

"Why? Won't you help me understand why?" There was a pleading note in her voice.

Gabriel looked up, and she gasped at the stark sorrow she saw on his face. "Of what purpose would that be?" He raked a hand over his face. "Other than dragging out the inevitable."

"It is important to me," Birdie replied. "You may shirk your responsibilities, but I won't. I'd like to have the chance to form a school for the children here." And get my marriage to work, she added mentally.

Gabriel stared. "A school! But why?"

"I want to help Eilidh and Ally and the remaining women. I promised them. I can't just desert them now."

Her husband shook his head in disbelief. "I do not know who they are."

"If you'd expressed some interest in your people here, you'd know who I am talking about."

He raised a weary hand. "They're not my people."

Birdie couldn't stop shaking her head at his stubbornness. She picked up a book. "It is going to be my turn to throw a book at you," she warned.

A ghost of a smile flitted over his face. "What do you expect me to do?"

Birdie blinked. Was he giving in? "Nothing terrible, or that takes too much effort. Show some interest in this place and the people. Work yourself through the ledger or hire a steward. And"––she tilted her chin up––"have tea with me. Converse with me. Get to know me. I promise you; I am a kind, decent person. At least, I attempt to be one most of the time." She smiled self-consciously. "Take walks with me. The coast outside is spectacular. Don't perpetually hide in that tower of yours."

Gabriel's hand hovered at the door latch. He visibly struggled to respond to her suggestions. After a moment, he drew a deep breath. "One month?" he asked.

"Yes."

He gave a curt nod. "Very well, ma'am," he said before he stepped out into the corridor. He turned once more, throwing her a penetrating look. "I already know that you are a kind, decent person. In fact, it is a gross understatement. Which is the only reason I agree to give you this one month."

When Birdie snapped her mouth shut in astonishment, he'd already gone.

That had gone well, hadn't it?

The rest of the day, she pondered on what he could've possibly meant with "it was a gross understatement"—and remembered the feeling of his warm, silken fingers in her neck.

GABRIEL KNEW HE'D OVERREACTED.

But when he saw her standing there, holding his pistol from Waterloo, he'd lost all reason.

Seeing her in his room uninvited was more than an invasion of privacy.

It was as though she'd invaded his soul. Looking at his model, touching his things. His pistol. Prying and prodding at things that were none of her business.

No one had a right to do that. No one had a right to see the death and darkness that surrounded him. And he had no right to drag her down into his hellish hole. He recalled the look of terror in her eyes when he'd shouted at her. She'd nearly fallen down the stairs backwards. She could've broken her neck. This was the second time she'd fled from him after confronting him in this very room. What was it about her that made him shout at her?

He'd stared out of the window of his tower room and had seen the purple flowers beneath. He knew he had to make amends. So, he'd gone out, for the first time in years, and done something he'd never done in his entire life: picked flowers like a lovelorn schoolboy.

She'd been in her room and had told him to enter, and when he did, he nearly toppled over. She stood in her shift, and all he saw were the luscious curves of her body, the sweet arch of her neck.

He'd buttoned her dress with trembling fingers.

And now, he still felt the sensation on his fingers: the silky smoothness of her skin.

One month.

By George. What had he done? One month of leading a normal, married life. With a proper wife. Spending the afternoons with her, sipping tea, discussing Shakespeare. He felt himself breaking out in a sweat.

He did not know how to be a husband.

What a mystery that woman was. He could make no rhyme and reason out of her behaviour. Yet, her eyes were windows to her soul and expressed every nuanced emotion. They'd gone from fearful to apprehensive to humorous, then speculative, horrified, determined. It was only that last look she'd given him, with a tremulous smile on her lips, that he couldn't identify.

On one account, she'd been right; it had been good for him to be outside. The wind had swept through his stagnant brain and left him more clear-headed and refreshed than he'd been in years. He'd seen, for the first time with clarity, the state of the castle. His military mind assessed the strategic location of the place. It had surprised him how sweeping the fortress was. Some parts looked decrepit. It had left him curious to see more.

One could decide to leave the tower occasionally and, for example, take a walk outside the castle battlements.

One could also ask her to accompany him. Not all the

time. But, perhaps, once in a while. So he could see that look in her eyes again. Feel her little hand in his.

He shook himself. What was he thinking? It was out of the question. He'd agreed to one month. Very well. During that time, he'd simply have to stay out of her way as much as possible.

CHAPTER 13

The smell of coffee and freshly baked bread wafted through Birdie's nose. Her stomach growled.

The new cook had prepared an excellent breakfast with strong coffee, fresh bread, and eggs.

The table was set for two people, but only she was present.

"Good morning, Higgins," she said cheerfully as the old man doddered towards her with the coffeepot. She lifted her cup quickly before he poured the coffee over her eggs. "That will be all right, Higgins." She took the pot from him before he dripped it all over the carpet.

"Has the duke had breakfast yet?" she asked.

He squinted at her. "He must be in bed?"

"No. I asked whether he's broken his fast." She made an eating motion with her hand.

"Yes, he has a broken past," Higgins muttered.

Birdie gave up. "Say, Higgins, where do you sleep?" She pointed at him, and then placed both hands under her head, then lifted her shoulders and arms.

"What, me? Where I sleep? I sleep outside in the old guardroom."

"But why?"

"Why?"

"There's more than enough room here!" she shouted that so loudly that he understood.

"Yes, yes. But there are also ghosts."

Birdie shook her head impatiently. "No, there are not. Silly boys' tricks." She took him outside and showed him the sheet and the candle that she'd found the other night. "Here's your ghost. Someone is playing a trick on us."

Higgins scratched his head. "This is the ghost of Dunross castle?"

"It appears so, Higgins. You do not know who might be behind this?"

"Someone who is up to no good," he muttered. "There are ghosts a-plenty here. No point in creating new ones."

"Entirely my point, Higgins. The question remains, who would do this? And why?"

A look of alertness flashed through his watery eyes. "Someone who is trying to harm the duke."

"The duke!" Now, this was a new thought. Was this entire thing not aimed at Birdie, after all? "With this"––Birdie gestured at the sheet––"a child's prank?"

"Aye. It may also be a child."

Did Higgins have a point? Was the culprit a child? For it was certainly childish, no doubt about that.

"Come with me." She took him by the elbow and walked him down the stairs to the servants' hall. For the first time, the kitchen was full of life. It steamed, gurgled, bubbled and hissed. Mrs Gowan chopped, and a girl named Annie peeled vegetables. There was a perfectly respectable and thoroughly cleaned butler's room and pantry, made ready by the women the other day. It contained a simple but clean bed and a wardrobe.

"It is so much better here, don't you agree? It is also warmer here than outside."

Higgins scratched his head again. "You want me to sleep here?"

"Yes. And I want you to stop locking us in while you are outside."

"The old duke swore the place was haunted," he muttered. "Didn't come here often."

"What kind of man was he?" Perhaps she could get some information out of him. He didn't understand what she'd said and continued to ramble on.

"Maybe he was wrong. Like about so many other things. I have served three generations of dukes. The last one was the worst. And this one—" He paused and shook his head sorrowfully.

"What about this one?" Birdie prompted.

"He is a good man. But he is broken."

"Why?"

Higgins lifted a gnarly hand and patted it against his chest. "Too many ghosts here."

"Can you tell me about his ghosts?"

But Higgins's moment of clarity was over. He shook his head and muttered, "I must polish his shoes." Then he looked about. "It is warmer here. And the wind is not so loud. She wants me to sleep here. Aye, I will. Even if it is haunted."

Birdie looked after him thoughtfully as he shuffled away. Higgins certainly wasn't the one who'd pulled the prank with the ghost. Neither, she was certain, had it been Gabriel. She was certain he'd spoken the truth when he said he never set foot outside the castle.

She returned to her room and her eyes fell on the velvet purse on her dresser. It was bulging. Birdie opened it and gasped. It was filled to the brim with coins. She was certain she'd spent most of it on the servants.

Someone had refilled it. She searched for a note, but there was none.

Gabriel? It must be.

Her mind was in a whirl. She closed it and packed it away safely in a drawer.

The man was full of mysteries.

What ghosts were haunting him?

LATER, Birdie took a walk by the cliffs.

The water slapped onto the black, jagged rocks, foaming and gurgling. Mist rose from the ocean and wrapped the castle in a white, lacy veil.

She'd always loved the sea, but other than an excursion to Brighton one summer with Miss Hilversham and her friends, she'd had little opportunity to see the ocean.

She loved the sound of the waves on the beach and the redolent smell of salt, even the wild shrieking of the seagulls. The wind teased the hair out of her bun and whipped it across her face.

She wrapped her shawl around herself more tightly and wandered along the path.

From here, the view of the castle was magnificent. Proud. Indomitable.

She sat down in the grass and pulled some flowers. They were the same purple flowers that her husband had picked for her.

She heard the crunching of boots on the gravel and looked up.

There he was.

He was walking, deep in thought, his face averted. It had

become natural for him to hold his head crooked as if he wanted to shield people from the damaged side of his face.

Birdie scrambled up, and he came to a startled halt.

He turned in her direction and looked flustered, almost bashful, when he spotted her. "I didn't know anyone was here." A flush of dull red spread over his cheeks.

"You took my advice and went out in the fresh air. I am impressed." Birdie smiled at him.

"I wanted to see the castle from this perspective," he explained.

"It is magnificent."

He turned to share her view. "Yes, I suppose it is." His black hair tumbled over his brow. Birdie gazed at his profile, the expressive brow with an aquiline nose, a firm chin with a sensitive mouth. The scar almost touched the curve of his mouth. She longed to trace it with her finger. Maybe even press a kiss on it.

Now, where on earth had that thought come from? She drew in a shuddering breath and wrapped her arms around herself to prevent herself from doing anything foolish.

He looked at her sharply. "Are you cold?"

If truth be told, she was rather hot.

He took off his coat and placed it around her shoulders before she could say anything.

"Th–thank you." She inhaled the spicy, smoky, masculine scent of his leather jacket. Gabriel stood in front of her in shirtsleeves. Once more, the analogy of a pirate came to her.

"Did you ever wish to become a sailor?" Birdie blurted out the first thing that came to her mind.

"No. I would have made a poor naval officer. I don't have any sea legs at all. I am a landlubber through and through."

"Sometimes I wish I could board a ship and sail away. One can't help but wonder what horizon is beyond, where the sun meets the sea." Birdie pointed at the distance, where the sun dipped into the ocean.

Gabriel followed her gaze. "I suppose if you follow it long enough, you'll end in the Americas."

"It must be nice to be a man and to have the freedom to travel," Birdie said wistfully.

"Do you wish to travel?" He gave her an inquisitive look.

"Oh, yes. This is the farthest I've ever travelled. I am in the midst of a glorious adventure." She took a big breath of salty sea air.

"You think this is an adventure?"

Birdie opened her eyes wide. "Very much so. Look around you. What do you see?" She waved her hand about.

"A decrepit castle. A village full of grumpy people. Infernally damp weather and a girl who is shivering."

She uttered a short laugh. "I see a beautiful medieval castle, a cobalt blue ocean and a fairy tale meadow with purple flowers. There is much potential in this place."

"You seem to enjoy being here more than I."

"Perhaps that is because I am more curious about people and places than you are."

He did not respond to that.

"What happened that gave you this scar?" she heard herself say.

He stilled.

"I apologise. You don't have to tell me if you'd rather not." She turned back toward the castle.

"You have repeatedly accused me of not caring for the people here. I would like you to understand some things," Gabriel said in a low voice. "So that you don't think I am the monster many think I am."

Birdie held her breath.

"I was the captain of a light company in the second battalion, Coldstream Guards. We were a close-knit group of nearly fifty men. We'd fought many wars together: the Peninsula, Spain, Portugal. You wouldn't find a finer and more loyal bunch of men. Even though I was the youngest of the lot, I was their leader and captain. They trusted me with their lives." Gabriel looked at her with burning eyes. "And because they did, they are all dead now. Every single one of them. Because of me. Because they followed my command."

"It was a war. You couldn't have known of the consequences," Birdie whispered.

"It was my job to know," he snapped harshly. "I was their captain. I was their leader. They trusted me blindly. If I told them to go right, sending them straight into the jaws of hell, they did so without as much as blinking. None of them survived. Only me. I was lucky." Gabriel pointed at his cheek. "This is nothing compared to what happened to many others. When I woke up in the infirmary, everything was over. They were dead––and I survived."

Tears streamed down Birdie's face.

"So, you see, Birdie." Gabriel shook his head. "I can't ever lead men again. I lead them to death and destruction. People are better not to put their trust in me––including you."

THAT NIGHT, Birdie fell into a troubled sleep. She dreamt about a war she'd never seen; she heard the cannons, saw the blood on the battlefield. Amid everything was him. On his knees, weeping. A beautiful strain of music played over the scene of carnage.

Powerful, melancholic, divine music.

"How lovely," Birdie muttered, as she turned over in bed, pushing her head further into her pillow. The scene in her dream shifted. She now dreamt she was back at the seminary, and she was playing on a grand Broadwood piano.

Her friends stood around the piano, clapping. "How wonderfully you play, Birdie!" her friend Arabella exclaimed.

Birdie's eyes snapped wide open.

That was all wrong. One thing Birdie couldn't do particularly well was play the pianoforte. Birdie had no illusions about her own piano skills.

Yet the beautiful sound remained, the strands of music clear and sweet. The playing was not merely part of a dream after all.

Birdie scrambled up, pulled a scarf over her shoulders, and slipped out of her room.

The sound came from the drawing room.

Was that Beethoven?

Birdie tipped the door open with her fingertips.

Gabriel sat by the piano, his shirtsleeves rolled up, playing with intense concentration.

Birdie had never heard anything like it. Her hand went to her mouth.

He played with his head thrown back, his eye closed. The music swelled to a sweet crescendo before it fell to a final, resounding chord.

A single tear ran down Birdie's cheek. She sniffed and wiped it with her sleeve.

Gabriel whirled around in the piano chair and their eyes met.

He was still half dazed from playing.

"I vow I will never touch the piano again. That was divine." Birdie stepped into the room. "Why didn't you tell me you could play the piano so well?"

He ran a hand through his hair. "I thought I'd forgotten. It's been so long." He flexed his fingers. "But my fingers remembered."

"It was amazing. You play better than my friend Arabella,

and she is quite the pianist. You also tuned it yourself?" Birdie asked in wonder.

He let his fingers gently brushed over the piano keys. "When I was younger, I wanted to be a musician..." His voice seemed to come from far away. "My father was against it. He was a merchant, and he did not think it a lucrative vocation. He wanted me to take over the family business. I used to go to our neighbour's house and play on his piano. My father heard me through the window. When I saw him standing there, I thought, 'That's it! I will never get to touch a piano again.' He left without a word. But that evening, he returned with a pianoforte." His eyes glazed over in memory.

"And yet you ended up becoming a soldier. Why?"

"I knew I would never become the merchant my father wanted. I was realistic enough to know music wouldn't provide a sufficient income, either. So I enlisted. It turned out to be the biggest mistake of my life."

A silence settled between them. It was neither uncomfortable nor charged. Birdie thought of Gabriel as a little boy, sensitive and musically inclined, and how cruel it was that he ended up in muddy trenches defending his country. And how that experience had broken him.

She could've wept.

"Birdie."

She looked at him inquisitively.

She saw him take a breath before he said, quickly, as if he wanted it out before he regretted it, "I've been a fool. You've invested energy and effort into hiring servants and making this heap of stone a more comfortable and agreeable place to live. And all I did was berate you for it. You deserve thanks instead."

Birdie regarded him thoughtfully. "There is one way in which you can thank me," she replied.

His eye flew up to meet hers. "How?"

"You gave me one month to stay here."

He nodded.

"I want it to be a proper month. I want you there, behaving like a reasonable human being. Like a proper husband. All I am suggesting is that perhaps we could meet for breakfast, tea and supper and converse like reasonably civilised people. That is all I ask."

Gabriel sighed.

"Is it such an unreasonable demand?" Birdie asked.

"Why is that so important to you?"

"I never thought I'd be married." She smiled bleakly. "So, I'd like to pretend for a month everything is normal."

"I don't think I can do normal, Birdie," Gabriel whispered. "I am not at all certain what 'normal' is."

"Well, neither am I. Is anyone? Maybe it is what it is, and we decide for ourselves?"

He looked at the tips of his boots.

"I don't think what I am asking for is unreasonable," Birdie prompted. "We're married, after all."

He looked up, and their eyes met. One eye, granted, was covered by that piratical patch. But if one disregarded that, his remaining healthy eye was chestnut brown, fringed by dark eyebrows. He looked troubled.

Why? What was he so worried about?

"Conversing like reasonably civilised people." His Adam's apple bobbed up and down as he swallowed. Then he nodded curtly. "Very well," he said after a long silence.

"Wonderful!" Birdie clapped her hands together. "We start tonight with supper. I am so tired of sitting all by myself."

Gabriel hesitated, but then gave a curt nod.

"You will see that conversing with me is not as arduous as you fear. Though, I must say," Birdie added with a smile, "we've been doing that successfully the last half an hour. Conversing, I mean."

Gabriel's head went up. "You may be right."

When he smiled, the first genuine smile she had seen, she caught her breath. It lit up his face and made him look boyish, at least ten years younger. For one moment, she saw the glimpse of the man he really was. She saw that moroseness was not an inherent part of his personality.

This man, she realised, was fundamentally decent and kind. He could be everything a girl would wish for.

If he gave her the chance, she could be that girl.

CHAPTER 14

*G*abriel helped Higgins set up a table in the drawing
room. He'd dine with Birdie there in the evening.
By George, the thought of spending an entire
evening alone with her made him nervous. What had got
into him, agreeing to this supper? Yet her eyes had lit up,
pleased, so he must've done the right thing.

He raked his hand through his hair.

The drawing room would do. It had panelled walls of
cedarwood, dark green curtains, and heavy carpets. It was
the most comfortable room in the castle. The large hall
below was too cold and draughty, and the dining room was
uninhabitable. The brigade of women who'd invaded the
castle the other day had scrubbed the dining room to the best
of their abilities, but the room merely had a rickety table, and
chairs were missing altogether. He suspected that they'd been
used as firewood at one point, since he once saw the leg of a
chair in the fireplace. Who the deuce burned furniture,
and why?

Birdie was right. He'd not bothered to get involved in the
place. He'd kept himself safely locked in his tower room and

neither knew nor cared about what happened around him. His conscience nagged at him.

He'd never asked for this title, this position, this responsibility.

When the lawyers had descended on him in his abode in London, he hadn't been pleased. He'd even tried to decline the title, but that hadn't been possible.

"You're the last remaining issue of the late Duke of Dunross," they'd insisted. He would become duke, whether he wanted to or not. Then Higgins found him in a tavern, roaring drunk, and dragged him home, scolding him the entire way.

Thanks to Higgins, he hadn't touched alcohol since then. It was ironic, given that whisky was apparently what kept the old man alive.

When the town got wind that there was a new duke amongst their midst, invitations came flooding in: balls, concerts, and breakfasts. They'd hounded him. So, he'd fled to Scotland. It had worked well. He'd not received a single letter here. The only letter he'd found was the one in his military uniform. Crumpled, wet and muddy. "It would please me to see you married, son," his father had written. He had already been dead by the time Gabriel had received the letter.

So, he'd married Miss Burns. Somewhat late, but he'd married her. He'd always told himself it was because it had been his father's last request of him.

Gabriel had never really considered himself to be the marrying kind. He had intended to remain a bachelor and to spend his life serving in the army, dying honourably on the battlefield.

Fate had decided something else for him.

Fate had wanted him to be a duke.

He now had a duchess as well, with whom he was

supposed to converse tonight. If he were honest with himself, it terrified him.

After he helped Higgins move the table to the drawing room, he returned to his tower.

He immediately noticed something was wrong.

Narrowing his eyes suspiciously to two slits, he surveyed the room. Something looked different here. It also smelled odd. Then it hit him. The moldy, dusty smell was gone. It smelled clean. Of lemon, beeswax and... was that lavender? His gaze fell on a bowl with pot-pourri on a side table next to his bed. His grey woollen blanket was gone, and in its stead, there was a thick mattress covered with a white, crisp linen sheet, a neatly folded blanket, and a fluffy down pillow. Where had this small oaken box come from? Where was his pile of clothes?

The fireplace, cleaned of ash, gleamed, and the grate was polished. A thick, quilted blanket covered his bed. Someone neatly stacked his books on a little table, which hadn't been there before. Was that frilly thing a lampshade?

Someone had dusted, cleaned, and sorted the room in the one hour he'd left. He knew who it was, even if she was the one who'd merely given the order.

Lavender! In a soldier's room!

Where was his pistol? His eyes flew to the windowsill. Someone had washed his brushes and neatly lined them up there; the tin cans next to them were sorted according to colour.

His pistol was gone.

This, Gabriel decided, was beyond the pale.

It was simply and utterly intolerable.

. . .

BIRDIE HAD BEEN busy the entire afternoon working in the library. With the help of the women, they'd taken every single book off the shelves and given it a good, thorough clean. To the shock of the maids, Birdie herself had tied an apron around her dress and had taken a rag in hand.

"These books are precious," she'd told them. "Stack them all on the floor over here. I will dust them myself." This is what she had been doing for the third day in a row. Her plan was to sort and catalogue them eventually, but for now, she wanted to put the library to order so it could serve as a schoolroom.

Birdie wiped the books down with the rag and stacked them into organised piles. There was quite a collection of Shakespeare and many books on history and geography. She pulled out a universal almanack from 1713, which, though outdated, might prove useful; Burns' *Letters on the Improvement of the Mind*, which she pushed back into the shelf; a book on etiquette and ah—the greatest treasure of the library: a primer for little children, to teach them their ABCs.

"This, ladies and gentlemen, is worth more than Shakespeare," declared Birdie from where she stood on top of the ladder, clutching the book happily in her hands. In the furthest corner of the shelf, she spied an original edition of *Robinson Crusoe*. "This one, too." She could read it to the children. They would love it. She tucked the geography book and the almanack under one arm, and, poking her tongue out of the corner of her mouth, reached for the *Crusoe*. Just as her fingertips brushed the leather book spine, the door flew open.

"Birdie!" Gabriel roared.

The door crashed against the ladder, which wobbled dangerously. Birdie reached out to clutch it, but because she had the books tucked under her arm, they toppled down, and that simply couldn't happen. They were too precious.

Trying to catch them, her fingers groped the empty air; the ladder wobbled, wobbled some more, and she went down with a crash—right on top of Gabriel, who never saw her coming.

She felled him neatly with a swoop and caught the primer.

Her body crashed on top of his, crushing the air out of both their bodies. "Oof!"

He'd smacked his head on the floor with a crack and lay there, his eye closed.

Birdie gasped for breath. Why didn't he move? "Oh, dear." She prodded Gabriel in the arm with the book. "I hope I haven't killed you," she gasped. She leaned forward to look at his face. His black hair tumbled over his aquiline forehead. She studied his lips. His lower lip was fuller than his upper lip. His eye was closed, and the eyepatch had slipped a bit.

Dare she look at what was beneath it?

Her finger crept upward slowly and hovered next to the patch. Just as she was about to touch it, his other eye popped open.

Startled, she withdrew, but his hand whipped up and gripped hers in an iron grasp.

She noticed his hard masculine body against hers, that smell of leather and smoke. It bewildered her senses.

"I was just about to—check—whether you were still alive," she babbled. She still lay on top of him, the primer in one hand, now pressed against his chest.

Gabriel was evidently not dead because he was breathing rather heavily. Birdie realised she was crushing the poor man. She'd have scrambled up, but his arms were clasped around her like iron bands.

She felt an odd stirring in the pit of her stomach.

"Can you please say something? You're awfully quiet and there's a glazed look in your eye," she said breathlessly.

"I'm fine." His voice was thick. He cleared his throat and loosened his grip.

"And your head?" She scrambled off him and backed away to put as much distance between them as possible. He sat up and shook his head.

"My head, ma'am, as previous wars have proven, is thicker than stone and impossible to crack." He adjusted the eye-patch.

"I'm glad." Birdie stared at him and clutched her primer, as if to ward him off. Something had happened that she couldn't interpret. A sizzling. A spark. A tingle as if the blood in her veins had turned to champagne bubbles. Birdie cleared her throat. "What was it you wanted?"

Gabriel looked at her blankly. Then a look of thunder shadowed his face. "Oh. Yes. I wanted something. You had my room cleaned!"

Birdie picked up the books and held them in her arms. "It was about time. Three maids went in and came out with five buckets of pitch-black water. You should've seen it."

Her husband folded his arms. "I thought I'd made myself clear: I don't want anyone in my room."

"Yes. I gave the orders that no one should disturb you. Which is why they cleaned after you left."

"No. I mean that not a single living, breathing, soul should enter my room. Ever." He jutted out his chin. "You touched and moved my possessions, and now some of my things have been moved or are missing. My pistol is gone."

"How excel—I mean. I do not know what happened to your blasted pistol. I gave instructions to the maids to work carefully and quickly. I gave the order not to remove anything aside from dust, dirt and cobwebs."

"But someone must've moved it!" Gabriel gave a frustrated huff.

To avoid his gaze, Birdie shuffled the books in her arms,

rearranging them. "You probably did so yourself," she said dismissively. "Sometimes we move things without thinking."

He threw her an irritated look. "I forbid anyone, including you, to touch my pistol. And I want everything in my room to be returned to its original state. Every. Single. Thing."

"Certainly. Your wishes shall be respected, Your Grace. Shall I instruct the maids to return each little speck of dust and grime? I'll tell them to shake out their rags there."

"Birdie." He gave an exasperated laugh and felt the back of his head.

"Oh, dear. Do you have a bump on your head?"

"I'm fine." Gabriel continued to rub his head.

Birdie lifted her hands to touch the back of his skull. His black curls were as soft as silk. This sizzling feeling pulsated through her. Again, there was an odd look on his face. She dropped her hands quickly.

"Look at the library, isn't it a gorgeous room now that it's clean?" she babbled. "It took four maids to carry the heavy carpet outside. Now we can see that it is Persian and quite valuable! I daresay this room is becoming my favourite by far. But look, how late it is! I need to get changed and ready for supper tonight. Do not forget. We dine at seven." Birdie gave him a last smile and promptly left, with the books under her arms.

Gabriel exhaled a shaky breath.

What the deuce had just happened? And he wasn't thinking of the library and the cleaning. Truth be told, he couldn't care less now. He had more imminent, disturbing problems. His heart still hadn't calmed down from the staccato it had hammered into his chest when Birdie had fallen on top of him. It was a sensation that he'd enjoyed rather more than he'd cared to admit. For one moment, he'd thought she was about to kiss him. Suddenly, there was nothing he wanted more. Zounds. When he'd opened his eye and gazed into her hazel ones, he almost kissed her.

Dash it. Why hadn't he?

He felt uncomfortably hot and bothered by the entire episode and had completely forgotten what he'd wanted from Birdie.

His pistol. It was all about his pistol. Where the deuce was it?

He took a step back and stumbled over a ghostly figure by the window, half-hidden by heavy brocade curtains. He uttered a muffled oath and grappled with it, only to discover it wasn't human, but a construct of broom and linen sheets.

The devil! Did the entire house conspire to bring him down?

Just at that moment, Higgins entered.

"Higgins!" Gabriel bellowed. "What is the meaning of this?"

"Beg your pardon, Your Grace," Higgins mumbled as he hobbled into the room. "It's a ghost."

"A ghost!"

"A ghost to scare the other ghost."

"Higgins. You're not making any sense."

"Aye, Your Grace. The other ghost was sitting on the fence." Higgins took the sheet and broom from Gabriel and set it up again. "Outside."

Gabriel shook his head. Had the old man lost his mind entirely?

"It's my own idea," the man boasted. "The best way to fight ghosts is with ghosts, especially if they aren't actual ghosts."

Gabriel pressed his fingers against his temples and massaged them. "Higgins."

"Oh, Your Grace. What to do with the painting?" Higgins pointed at the fireplace. Gabriel looked up. Only now he saw that above the mantle was a gaping space where the old duke's portrait had hung. "Her Grace insisted on taking it down."

The painting lay on the floor so that the old duke's haggard visage grimaced at the ceiling. Gabriel looked down at him. He hadn't noticed it there and would've stepped right on his face had Higgins not stopped him. He'd never known the man who'd left him with this inheritance. But he knew he had been a bad sort of man, grossly neglecting his estate and people. Not that he was much better, his conscience whispered. Had he ever bothered to inquire into the state of his estate? The tenants and their welfare? He tugged at his collar. And blast it, why was he still so infernally hot?

"What do you suggest doing with it, Higgins?" He looked down at the portrait cluelessly.

"What I'd do with it?" Higgins tilted his head sideways.

"Yes."

"I'd burn it," Higgins muttered. "The man deserved no better."

For a moment, Gabriel was speechless. "And yet you served the man loyally for what? Twenty years?"

"Twenty-three years, five months, six days and three hours. Then he kicked the bucket." Higgins bared his yellowed teeth in something that was supposed to be a grin. Then he pulled himself up proudly. "We Higginses have always served the Dukes of Dunross."

"So you said." Shame, really, that this Higgins was the last of his kind. Gabriel contemplated for a moment, then said, "Well, Higgins. Do what you must. If Her Grace doesn't want to see the man's visage, then so be it. Burn it."

Higgins' face lit up with delight. "Aye, Your Grace." He turned to leave.

"Oh, and Higgins," Gabriel called after him. "I hope you don't burn my painting when you outlive me. If they ever make one of me."

Higgins' laughter cackled through the corridors as Gabriel returned to his room to ponder on the impact this afternoon had on his sanity.

GABRIEL STRODE up and down in front of the window, hands clasped behind his back, and wondered where Birdie could be. She hadn't forgotten, had she?

Tugging at his cravat, he couldn't remember the last time he'd dressed up like this. He was conscious that the clothing was not the newest fashion. Dash it, he didn't even know what the newest fashion was. Weren't these lacy cuffs something that his grandfather had worn in his time? The lace hung over his wrists, and he shook it away impatiently. A man couldn't pick up anything without the bothersome lace in the way. He was a military man. He preferred simple, clean-cut, no-nonsense clothes.

He paced. He'd been half as nervous before his wedding. Dash it all. *Get a grip on yourself, Gabriel. It's just supper.*

Footsteps sounded at the entrance. He jumped.

She was here.

Birdie was dressed in a dark blue gown and scarf that brought the colour out of her eyes. Her hair was parted in the middle and done up, some strands teased out to frame her face, and the candlelight highlighted the auburn colour of her hair.

He gaped at her. What had she said? That she didn't have the looks? He almost snorted. Then he remembered his manners. "Good evening," he said politely. He pulled out a chair and gestured for her to approach.

Birdie sat. "This is very fine. I see Higgins has lit the candles. And oh! The flowers!" She jumped up again, went over to the window and smelled the flowers in the vase. They were the same purple flowers he'd picked for her the other day. No other flowers were growing in this place. It relieved him that she seemed to like them.

Higgins came stumbling into the room, nearly dropping the soup tureen. Luckily, Gabriel reacted quickly and caught it before it fell out of his hands. "Thank you, Higgins. We can serve ourselves."

"It's mock turtle soup," Higgins explained. "And I shall serve, Your Grace." It was as though he'd remembered his role, and even though his hands shook, he ladled soup into their bowls without spilling.

Then he bowed and left the room.

"Higgins certainly is an institution on his own." Gabriel looked at his retreating figure, shaking his head. "I offered him retirement with sufficient funds. He could live in his own place, comfortably. But he refused. Said it was a tradition for the Higgins butlers to serve the Dukes of Dunross until their very last day." He frowned. "He said it would be a shameful legacy for him to retire before that."

Humour sparkled in Birdie's eyes. "Higgins will outlast us all. He'll still be around when this place is a mere ruin," she said.

Supper was excellent. Cook had made them fowl, with a variety of side dishes and dessert. Gabe supposed it tasted good, but it was all lost on him. Birdie was encompassing his entire attention.

When Higgins served syllabub in dainty glasses, Birdie spooned it with relish, but Gabriel pushed his glass away.

"If you're not eating that, I will," Birdie said and reached for it.

His wife certainly knew how to enjoy food.

His wife. It was the first time he had thought of her as his wife, and he discovered he liked it. He was surprised with what ease they conversed. Her face was animated when she talked, and she had a tic of pushing her spectacles up the nose even though there was no need for it. It was more habit than anything else. Around her neck, on a chain dangled a ring. The wedding ring that had been too big for her.

Toying with the spoon in his coffee cup, Gabriel realised with a jolt how much he liked her. She had a fine sense of humour, a strong sense for the practical, and a kind, warm heart. She was talking now about her old school, Miss Hilversham's Seminary for Young Ladies, and the pranks she and her friends had played there.

"How odd. My friend Arabella wished that night that each of us marry dukes. Three of us did. Don't you think that is a strange sort of coincidence? Or do you think the wishing well had true powers and made it happen?"

"I don't believe in the supernatural," he heard himself say. "Though there is so much more out there in this world than we can understand."

"Oh! Speaking of supernatural." She leaned forward, an impish glint in her hazel eyes. "Did you know that Dunross Castle is haunted?"

"Hm. Yes. They say a morose, disfigured man haunts the tower room." He smiled wryly.

"You should never talk of yourself in those terms," Birdie scolded. "You are scarred, but not disfigured."

"I beg to disagree."

"Well, I must say, that eyepatch of yours is rather frightful, and makes you look so much more terrifying than you are." She studied his face so intently that he had to keep himself from squirming in the chair. "But what I meant was a ghost on the battlement."

"The battlement?" he echoed.

"Yes. I found it very odd because it appeared to be of the same kind that I and my friends used to create when back at school. A makeshift sheet with holes."

He frowned. "Higgins keeps babbling about ghosts. He even set one up in the library."

She uttered a low laugh. "I know. Higgins thinks it will scare the other ghost away."

"Are you saying that someone purposefully attempted to frighten you?"

"It appears so. But to what purpose? And why?" Birdie leaned on her hand. "Maybe we have it all wrong and that the ghost serves a different purpose entirely." She frowned. "Because the fake ghost isn't walking every night, but only on some. I am keeping track of it, you see. It may be a sign, or similar. A flag, maybe."

"What kind of sign do you mean?"

"If only I knew! It is a secret I am determined to discover. Even if it turns out to be a mere child's prank." She hesitated before adding, "Did it ever occur to you that the people in the village have no great love for us—particularly for you?"

He sighed. "It has never bothered me since we never see each other. But yes. The old duke did not treat them well. His steward died under mysterious circumstances."

"And you never installed a new steward."

He toyed with his cup. "No. McAloy, the reverend, tells me he handles things for me. He is respected in the village."

"It might be a good idea to have a proper steward," Birdie replied, and her chin jutted forward stubbornly.

"I am sure you have someone in mind." He leaned back in his chair.

Her lips pressed down as if to repress a smile. Gabriel

thought again of this afternoon, and of how close he got to kiss those lips.

"I might." Birdie smiled at him, and his heart jumped. "This was a lovely dinner," she added.

"Yes," he said lamely, "it was nice."

Birdie excused herself and left the room, and he exhaled. He hadn't noticed he'd been holding his breath.

Quite ridiculously, he was already looking forward to spending another evening with her.

CHAPTER 15

*B*irdie's days were suddenly busy. After having inspected the old school building in the village, she'd concluded that the only thing one could reasonably do was tear it down. The roof had fallen in, there was no fireplace, it was pitifully cold, and there was mold on the walls. It was not a safe place for children to learn.

"This will not do at all," Birdie had said. She marched back to the lower courtyard of the castle and investigated the buildings there.

There was the chapel. Next to it were stables, a smithy, and another building which must have been servants' quarters in medieval times. Edifices that once must have served as the pantry, buttery, and bakery had been moved into the keep throughout the centuries. Most buildings had doors and windows missing. One bigger building may have served as a servant hall. It was now a storage room full of crates and old furniture.

"This one." Birdie turned to a group of women with a nod. They carried brooms, buckets, and rags. "This will be our school."

When cleaned, painted, and furnished, it would be a spacious, functional schoolroom. Until then, she could teach the children in the library. She helped the women dust and scrub the place. Pleased with her day's work, yet with tiredness weighing down heavily in her bones, she returned to the main hall.

GABRIEL FOUND Birdie asleep on the recamier in the drawing room. The fire had gone out. Her head rested on one arm; her hand curled like a child's. She looked innocent but troubled in her sleep. There were dark shadows under her eyes. Dust clung to her shoes and clothes.

He looked at her helplessly.

What a brave soul she was.

A fighter.

A heart full of kindness and generosity.

She deserved better than this. She deserved better than him. He was too broken.

He pulled off her dusty shoes and placed them by the door. He re-lit the fire and picked up the blanket that had fallen on the floor and carefully draped it around her. He reached out with a shaking hand and tucked an errant strand of hair off her forehead. Maybe it was the smooth, silken touch of her skin. The long brown lashes that curled on her skin. The warm scent of lavender that filled his nose. The lush curve of her mouth. Something stirred in him, deeply. Without thinking, he bent over her, inhaling her scent. His mouth went dry.

Suddenly, her eyes popped open.

He held his breath. He feared the look that surely would enter her eyes. The look of terror. Of disgust.

But her gaze merely rested on him. There was no

surprise, only acknowledgement that he was here. Her eyes were dreamy and lit with golden flecks in her green-brown irises.

He drowned in them.

She reached out her hands, one on each side of the face, touching him there. Pulling him down.

She kissed him. As lightly as a feather.

DAZED, he walked down the dark corridor toward his lonely tower room.

It had been but a dream. The power of the mind. An illusion. He'd desired her, so he'd imagined kissing her.

She was still there, sleeping, dreaming, never knowing he'd been there.

Then why did he still feel her gentle touch on his marred cheek?

Why did his lips tingle?

BIRDIE HAD DREAMT a prince had entered the room. He was beautiful and kind. He'd tucked a blanket about her when she shivered, pulled off her shoes and re-kindled the fire. He'd caressed her cheek with gentleness as if she were the most precious thing he'd ever seen in his life.

She'd felt taken care of.

Safe.

Because she'd wanted to see her prince's face, she'd opened her eyes and kissed him. It had been sweet, warm, and light. She'd felt a happiness course through her she'd never felt before.

It had felt right.

Everything will be all right, she thought, as she turned, curled back into her pillow, and slept.

CHAPTER 16

"Your Grace," Higgins gasped. "The castle is invaded by children."

Gabriel dropped the book he'd been reading and stared at Higgins. He must truly hallucinate now.

"Come and see for yourself."

Indeed, as he hurried down the corridor, he heard the babble of what could only be correctly pinpointed as children's noises.

What on earth?

The chatter increased. It came from the library, which Birdie had insisted on refurnishing.

Without thinking twice, he burst into the room.

Immediate silence descended as eleven heads turned towards him in various states of astonishment.

There was Birdie, standing in the middle of a circle of approximately ten children who sat cross-legged on the floor, their chalkboards on their laps. They stared at him with open mouths.

Gabriel stood shell-shocked; he expected them to burst

into shrieks, tears and hysterics, for the daylight that poured through the windows clearly shone on his face.

The Monster of Dunross in plain daylight.

He braced himself.

"Children, this is the Duke of Dunross. Get up and say, 'How do you do' to His Grace," Birdie instructed.

The children scrambled out of their chairs and chanted in unison, "How do ye do, Yer Grace."

Gabriel flushed. "Er. Hello." Turning to Birdie, he asked, "What is the meaning of this?"

Birdie folded her hands. "We have decided to open a village school. The children have received no education at all since the old schoolteacher left. Besides, the school building in the village is about to collapse. Since there is so much space here,"––she waved her hand about––"I thought it would be an excellent idea to set up the school in one of the outer buildings here."

"We?"

"Some women in the village and myself."

"I see."

"And today we have library day. We are choosing books to read for the week, aren't we, children?"

They nodded eagerly.

"Miss, may I ask a question?" a black-haired boy asked after he stood up.

"Miss?" Gabriel echoed.

"I thought it better to use my maiden name while I teach," Birdie explained. "To keep identities apart. And yes, Johnny, you may ask a question."

"If you please. What happened to your face?" Johnny sat down again and looked at Gabriel expectantly.

He felt his cheeks burn. "It is a war injury," he explained.

"You mean, sir—"

"Your Grace," Birdie interjected.

"Yes, miss. You mean, Your Grace, sir, that you were fighting in the war? Against the French Beast?"

"Er. Yes."

"That's bloody brilliant!"

A chorus of children's voices chimed in:

"How was it like?"

"Did ye see him yersel?"

"Are ye a hero?"

"Does yer face still hurt?"

"Did ye—"

They jumped up and crowded around Gabriel, who backed up against the door, ready to flee.

"Children, if you sit down and calm down, His Grace will tell you all about his experiences in the war," Birdie said.

He was going to do what? Gabriel stared at Birdie, aghast.

But Birdie sat down quietly in an armchair, folded her hands in her lap, and looked at him invitingly. He looked around and saw the expectation on the children's faces. Bright, shiny faces with eager eyes.

"We're ready, sir, Yer Grace," piped up a little boy. He had curly auburn hair, a peaky little face and only one arm. He sat down right in front of Gabe with crossed legs and looked at him with anticipation.

"It was Sunday, the 18th of June 1815," he heard himself say. "Do you know where Waterloo is?"

The children shook their heads.

"It's on the continent. Near Brussels." Gabriel looked at Birdie for help.

"We will look it up in the Atlas afterwards, children," Birdie chimed in. "Continue, Your Grace."

"Six nations were pitched against France. The coalition consisted of Prussia, the Netherlands, Hanover, Nassau, Brunswick and the United Kingdom. The Prussians were in rear-guard—" He interrupted himself. He battled with himself for one moment before he made up his mind. He gave a curt nod. "I shall have to show you. Come with me."

He strode out of the room before he changed his mind.

A general scramble and the quick patter of feet followed him.

Higgins had been right when he'd said the castle was invaded by children, he thought, as he opened the door to his tower. They spilled into his room and gathered in awe around his miniature model of the battleground. Never in his wildest dreams would he have imagined, as he rose from of bed this morning, that he'd be spending his afternoon showing his precious model to a group of village children.

He told them the story of Waterloo. It was the first time he had ever talked about it.

It felt oddly liberating.

As he spoke, he noticed the little one-armed boy hung on to his every word, looking at him with serious, big eyes.

"… and after the Prussians broke through the French right flank—over here—and the coalition vanquished the French Imperial Guard, it was clear the battle was won."

"What is this?" Tommy, the one-armed boy, asked.

"This is a farm called La Haye Sainte."

"And this here?" the boy pointed to another building.

He felt himself grimace. "This is Chateau Hougoumont." Even though he hadn't intended to elaborate on it, he heard himself say, "This is where we were stationed. The light company of the second battalion. Coldstream Guards."

"Coldstream Guards!" The boys' mouths dropped open with awe. Hero worship gleamed in their eyes. Gabriel shifted uncomfortably.

"How pretty the houses are," a little girl with brown locks said and touched a model roof.

"Careful, the colour's not yet dry," Gabriel said involuntarily as she pressed down a finger on the model.

"Does it really look like that? If we were to go there now, it would look exactly like this, yes? Yer Grace, sir?"

Gabriel felt a rushing go through his ears and the din of guns in the distance. From a distance, his voice said, "Hougoumont was entirely destroyed."

He felt Birdie's eyes on him. "I think we have taken up enough of his Grace's time," she said to the little ones. "Come now, children."

"But miss. The model's not finished. Yer Grace, sir, do ye need help? We can help paint the little trees," said Johnny and looked at Gabriel expectantly.

Gabriel felt helpless. How could anyone deny those pleading eyes?

The girl had picked up a pot of paint and a brush and coloured the meadow without much ado. Before he could blink, the other children joined in and busied themselves by painting or modelling figures from the clay lump he'd left on the side.

Birdie threw him an apologetic look.

Only one boy stood in the shadow by the door, hanging his head. Tommy.

"Come here, Tommy. You can help me paint the soldiers of the 95th Rifles," Gabriel said. The boy came over slowly. Gabriel picked up a brush and green paint and showed him how to paint the figure. "The 95th rifles had green uniforms, not red ones. So, you need to colour them with particular care."

"Aye sir, they were real special, right?" Gabriel held the figure while Tommy painted it.

When he looked over Tommy's head, his eyes met Birdie's.

They were huge, and warm, and luminous. The smile she gave on him was so bright it lit up the entire room.

As unorthodox as it all was, he was doing the right thing.

He felt his heart lighten.

IT HAD BEEN AN AMAZING AFTERNOON. Birdie could hardly believe what had happened. Gabriel had arrived and had talked to the children, even invited them to his abode to show them the model! Then he'd let them paint the remaining figures and landscapes. Even Birdie thought that they'd gone too far, that maybe they'd exhausted his patience. But no. He'd taken little Tommy under his wing and patiently helped him paint a figure. Her heart had melted seeing his dark head bent over the little boy's bright curly one. The child clearly hero-worshipped him. He'd clung to Gabriel the entire afternoon, painting not one, but three soldiers, which Gabriel allowed him to set in the middle of the scene.

"I want them to guard the gate," Tommy directed. "They are the bravest soldiers in the entire army. No one will get past them."

"They will ward off the entire French army single hand-edly," Gabriel had replied, and Tommy had beamed at him, and slipped his little hand into his big one.

He would make a wonderful father one day, Birdie thought.

The children, satisfied after such an eventful afternoon, thanked him one by one and left.

After they had gone, Gabriel remained standing by the window. There was a strain about his eyes, and he looked pale.

Birdie hesitated by the door. "I just wanted to say—what you did was wonderful. Thank you. Truly. The children will remember this for a long time."

He nodded curtly. He wasn't upset with her, was he?

"I—would like to invite you. For supper. Tonight," she blurted out. "To celebrate a special day. I can tell cook to prepare Soupe a la Reine, pheasant pie, and an apricot tart. Or would you prefer curried rabbit? Or something more traditionally Scottish?" She was definitely talking too much. And he was being altogether too quiet.

He raised his hands to his temples and rubbed them. "Curried pheasant is fine," he muttered.

Curried pheasant? He hadn't been listening at all, had he? She supposed Cook would have to improvise, then.

"I will see you later at supper? In the dining room, this time," she added, to make sure he went to the correct room. "Higgins has found the chairs, and the village carpenter has repaired them. They're as good as new!"

Gabriel nodded.

"Well then. I will see you in several hours."

He nodded again.

Birdie left to take a bath and to change into her prettiest dress. It was a sea green evening gown that Eilidh had magically refashioned. It fit her to perfection. Ally combed her hair up and managed to produce something akin to curls. For the first time in her life, Birdie felt pretty.

Cook had disapproved of the menu.

"It'll be haggis, neeps and tatties tonight or nuthin' at all," she said.

"But Mrs Gowan. We've had this so often already. Tonight is to be special."

The cook grumbled. "Tattie soup and mutton pie, then. And for dessert the leftover syllabub from th'other day."

"That sounds divine, Mrs Gowan," Birdie said.

When the candles were lit and the table was set, she waited for him eagerly. It was funny how her heart hammered in that manner. Was this what happiness felt like?

A sizzling feeling of excitement that coursed through her veins?

If Cecily Burns had known about Gabriel––that he was not only a duke, but a kind, caring one, with fundamental decency and integrity—would she have still insisted on her madcap scheme? The thought of Cecily immediately quenched her feeling of happiness.

Deep guilt burned inside her at her own deception. She needed to come clean with Gabriel, who still thought she was Miss Burns.

Someone knocked on the door, and she jumped.

It was Higgins.

"Beg your pardon, Your Grace," he said. "Can I serve the soup already?" He was carrying the soup tureen.

"Do wait, Higgins. His Grace hasn't arrived yet."

Higgins set the tureen on the table. "Aye, he's gone to bed," he muttered.

"I don't think so." Birdie bit her lips. Higgins had misunderstood her, hadn't he? He said he was coming.

Higgins looked at her with watery eyes. "Will you be waiting, Your Grace?"

"Of course." She smoothed her skirt down with skittish hands. Why wasn't he coming? He probably needed more time to get ready.

After half an hour had passed, she sent Higgins to check on him. But he was sitting in the chair by the door, snoring.

An hour later, with the soup entirely cold, Birdie felt a sinking stone of disappointment in her stomach.

He wasn't coming.

He either had forgotten, which was unlikely. Or he'd simply changed his mind. If so, he could've sent her a message. Or even better, he could've told her so himself.

She felt something well up inside her, which she blinked away quickly.

"Well then, I shall simply have to eat the good food on my own," she decided, sat down, and went to work. "Before it goes to waste."

It didn't taste half as good eating it alone. Perhaps she could send up a tray with some leftovers, but then she wasn't certain he deserved it after letting her sit in the cold like that.

What a difficult man he was.

She stared into the fire, suddenly overwhelmed with a feeling of defeat and sadness.

Why was she sitting here all on her own, feeling sorry for herself? Birdie got up and marched by the sleeping Higgins.

If he wasn't coming to her, then she would go to him.

Simple, really.

BIRDIE KNOCKED TIMIDLY on the door of the tower room. It was hard to believe that only several hours ago, the place was swarming with children who'd cheerfully hopped in and out of the room.

Now the closed, heavy oaken door stared at her as if it concealed Blackbeard's den.

Birdie shifted the lamp to the other hand and pushed down the handle. It wasn't locked.

The room inside was entirely dark. Not even the fireplace was lit.

"Gabriel?"

No answer.

She lifted her lamp. His bed was empty. She swung the light to the other side. No one there.

Was he on the way down to the dining room? Had they passed each other without noticing?

Confused, Birdie dropped the lamp. Then she saw the shadow on the floor.

In front of the extinct fireplace, a figure huddled, crouched together into a tight ball. His arms covered his head, and he shivered.

"Gabriel! What happened!" Birdie set down the lamp on the table and rushed to him.

Gabriel muttered something unintelligible and shook his head.

She reached out and gently touched his shoulder. He didn't react. She grabbed him harder and shook his shoulder. "Gabriel. Are you ill?" His hands and forehead seemed hot. But was it fever?

"Gabriel." She shook his arm. Was he sleeping?

"To the left, not to the right," he muttered. He looked up, and his face was wet with tears.

"What is to the left? Gabriel?"

"My men. It should've been the left."

"I don't understand." Birdie shook her head.

"I told them to hold the right while the others defended the gate. They trusted me. They followed me without question. They shouldn't have. They held the right, like I told them to. And then..." His body shook with sobs.

"And then?"

"And then the French shelled the house with the entire battery of howitzers they had available. One moment they were there. Then next they were gone. Every single one of them. My entire company. Fifty men. Blown to smithereens. And then a burning beam crashed on me and knocked me out. But I wasn't granted the mercy of death. Do you understand?" He sat up and there was a wild light in his eye. "I am the only one who survived the massacre after I sent my men to their deaths. And then they gave me this." He held out his hand, which was clenched around a round piece of metal.

Birdie took it. The Waterloo medal.

Birdie grabbed his hand and pressed it tight. Tears ran

down her face. "You told them to do what you believed was right. I've never been in a war, but I can imagine one must make decisions on the spot, based on the surrounding facts. You assessed the situation and decided the men were better off defending the right. That doesn't make you responsible for what happened. You couldn't have known they'd blow Napoleon's entire battery right at you."

"I should've known." Gabriel's lips were cracked and dry. "It was my job to know." He leaned his head against her shoulder.

"But you also had superiors? Was it your choice to be there, to begin with?"

"No. We were ordered to hold the farm at all costs."

"So, you were following orders."

He looked at her as if seeing her for the first time. "Yes, I was following orders."

"Whose orders were you following?"

"General Sir James McDonell. He was holding the gate."

"And while he was holding the gate, he said you and your men were to defend the right wall."

"Hold the flank at the right. Don't let the French break through. Whoever wins the farm, wins the war."

"And that is what you did. Because you followed orders. That's what you do in a war. You were an excellent captain. You held the farm. You won the war. Whoever wins the farm, wins the war, you said. Well, you won the war."

"Carnage does not adequately describe what happened there." Gabriel looked blindly at the ceiling, as if reliving the scene.

He buried his head in her lap, and Birdie held him as he wept. She felt such sorrow for the man who felt responsible for the deaths of so many. Hot tears rolled down her cheeks.

It was getting cold. The candle tapered out. Birdie's legs

cramped, and she shifted around uncomfortably on the hard floorboards.

Gabriel got up, took a blanket from the bed, wrapped her in it, and lifted her onto the bed. Then he re-lit the fire in the fireplace.

Shadows flitted over the wall, and the wind howled over the tower. Despite the eeriness of the place, Birdie felt safe with him.

He knelt by the bed and dug his face into her lap. "Stay with me tonight." His words were muffled in the blanket.

She lifted his face in her hands and looked straight into his troubled dark eye. Without thinking, she reached out and touched the side of his face.

She pulled his face toward her.

She felt the hard bumps and ridges of the scars under her fingers. Her fingers moved to his patch. He did nothing to prevent her from lifting it.

His eyelid was closed. The lashes melted into the skin. Nothing terrible at all. An eye that was forevermore sleeping. That was all.

Without thinking, she pressed her lips to it.

Goodness, it shot through her. How she loved this man. She'd realised it when she saw him with Tommy on his lap. A warm tenderness had flooded through her, combined with a feeling of pride and a fierce joy like nothing she'd ever experienced before. She knew that, despite his demons, he was a man worthy of loving. If only he would let her.

"Yes," she whispered. "I will stay with you tonight."

CHAPTER 17

*T*he next day, the children didn't come.

Birdie did not notice until much later because she'd spent the entire day in her own dreamworld, with a vapid smile on her face.

He'd told her so much more, in the darkness of his room. He'd bared his soul to her. All the shadows, the terrors, the terrible images that had haunted him, that had kept him imprisoned. By finally allowing her in, she could help him carry his burden. She knew such a task was precious beyond words.

He'd also told her other things. Sweet things that he'd whispered, endearments that she'd never heard or read about before. Caresses that left her shivering with delight.

She'd left him sleeping in the morning, and there had been a peaceful look on his face; the kind that little children have when they have fallen into a deep, healing sleep.

It was a sunny day, and Birdie worked in the kitchen garden, pulling out weeds.

She held a handful of purple flowers in her hands, remembering the timid offer Gabriel had given her after their first quarrel. She'd pressed those flowers between sheets in her books to keep as a memento.

Birdie lifted her face to the sun.

Everything would be well. She felt it down to her bones. A feeling of warmth and peace flooded through her.

He was healing. She was gradually putting this place together. Maybe, one day, they would have children.

Then it struck her. Children!

Where were the children? She'd entirely forgotten that she was to teach them this morning.

Birdie scrambled up and ran back to the courtyard. That was when she noticed the silence. Where was everyone? Why was the schoolroom empty? Weren't the women supposed to clean today? Come to think of it, she hadn't seen Ally, either.

"Higgins!" She found the old man polishing wine glasses in the hall. No other person was in sight. "Where is everyone?"

He looked up with watery eyes. "They didn't come. Cook never came either. Had to eat porridge again." He looked displeased. "Left you a plate for breakfast." He pointed at a lone porridge bowl on the table.

She looked at Higgins, shocked, realising only now that she hadn't eaten all day, and not noticed.

"But why?"

"Because the people here have always had bad blood towards the Dukes of Dunross. It's a bad place. Haunted by evil."

Birdie let go of his arm and shook her head. She would go down to the village herself and talk to them.

. . .

A STRANGE QUIET had settled over the village. The street, usually full with playing children, was empty. No one was working in the gardens. No one came out to greet her.

She knocked on Eilidh's door and saw the curtain move inside, but no one opened the door.

"Eilidh? Tommy?" she called, and walked around the house, where sometimes the children played in the garden. No one was there. Birdie looked around, confused.

What was happening? Where had everyone gone?

"Psst. Miss. Your Grace," a little voice whispered from underneath the blueberry bush. It was Eilidh's youngest, Elsa.

"Elsa. Thank goodness. What is happening? This is so strange. Where has everyone gone?" She pulled the girl behind the trees so no one would see them from the house. "Why haven't you and the others come to school? Where is your mother?"

"We are not to go to school anymore, Your Grace, miss," said the little girl. She dropped her eyes. "Father forbade it."

That Logan McKenna. He was Eilidh's husband and Tommy and Elsa's father, and a definite good-for-nothing. Birdie felt fury flash through her. "But there is no sense in it whatsoever! Why object to having his children receive education, for free?" she exclaimed.

"It's not just my father, Your Grace, miss. The parents of the others as well. They don't like it. They want us to work."

"Work!" Birdie ground her teeth.

"Aye, there's lots of work."

"And your mother? Why hasn't she come, with the others?"

Elsa merely looked at her with sad eyes.

"Elsa. You're a good girl. I need to find a solution to this. Don't disobey your parents if they've told you not to come to the castle. Tell your mother I miss her and Ally, and I hope she changes her mind and continues to work for me. There is much work left, and enough payment for everyone."

"Aye Your Grace, miss."

The girl walked back to the house, changed her mind, scampered back to Birdie, pressed her face into her skirt in a fierce hug, and then ran away.

Birdie returned to the castle, her mind in turmoil.

Looking up, she saw a white sheet flutter on the barbican. Someone had put up the makeshift ghost again. This time in the middle of the day.

Fury shot through her. "I will uncover what is behind this all if it's the last thing I ever do," she muttered and stomped up the path to the castle.

SHE SMELLED it before she saw it. The pungent, acrid smell of something burning. Black smoke billowed to the sky. Birdie quickened her steps until she ran the last stretch into the castle courtyard. Stunned, she stared at the fire and smoke emerging from the windows of their schoolroom.

"Heaven help us, the castle is burning," Higgins gasped as he stumbled down the stairs from the main hall.

She rushed forward without thinking, but Higgins caught her by the arm.

"What are you doing, woman?"

"What if someone is inside?" Birdie shouted. She shook off Higgins's hand and ran to the entrance.

"It is too late for anyone who is inside," Higgins said.

"Higgins, get help, call the duke, fetch the men from the village, we need water—" Birdie cut herself off as she spied a moving shape inside the burning room. "There's someone inside!"

What if it was one of the children? Horror overwhelmed her. She rushed forward, and without thinking, hurtled into the burning building. Smoke burned in her eyes; she teared up and could see nothing at all. She fell back, choking and coughing.

"Is anyone there?" she shouted. The desks and chairs were burning. With sudden clarity, she realised that someone must have thrown them in a heap in the middle of the room and set them on fire. The fire now licked at the wooden beams on the roof. With alarm, she realised the entire structure would collapse soon. She coughed and choked, and called out again, "Anyone? Is anyone here?"

From the farthest corner of the room, she heard a weak "Miss!" She edged around the burning pile.

There. Again. "Miss!"

"Tommy!"

The child huddled in a corner, his head on his knees. Birdie stumbled toward him and pulled him to her.

"Keep your head down," Birdie gasped, "and hold on tight to me." A cloud of black smoke engulfed them. Both coughed. She could no longer see where the door was. They would have to get up and run for it anyhow.

At that moment, the beam cracked and crashed on the floor.

They were trapped.

So this is how she was going to die. With someone else's child in her arms, trapped in a burning room. She didn't see her life flash by, but oddly enough, heard her friend Lucy's voice, sweet and clear: *"Remember this: things never are what they appear to be. You just have to have the courage to see things differently."*

Her friend, cheeky as she was, had a point. Birdie lifted her head with determination. She would not stay there and die just like that. Not without a fight. She saw that, even though the beam blocked the path, there was a little space on the other side--but not if they waited for long.

"Come. We have to go. Now." She grabbed Tommy and pushed him to the floor. "On your front. Crawl. Keep your head as low as possible. You can do this, Tommy!"

They crawled around the other side of the burning pile. The second beam cracked--it would come crashing down on them if they did not hurry. Birdie pushed Tommy along on the floor. They were almost there.

Almost.

The beam tilted downward.

Then a pair of muscular arms grabbed her and pulled her out.

BIRDIE CLUNG TO GABRIEL, tears running down her cheeks.

"Birdie!" Gabriel picked her up, carried her to the stairs, and set her down. He wiped her face gently with trembling fingers. "Are you hurt?" His voice cracked. His fingers roved over her body to check whether she was all right.

"I am fine, Gabriel. The boy? Where is he?" she gasped.

Little Tommy was in his mother's arms. Birdie was unsure when Eilidh had appeared, but she clung to her son, rocking him back and forth.

"Eilidh! Is Tommy hurt?"

The woman looked up with a wet face. "He is fine, Yer Grace. He is fine. Thanks to God. And to ye, Yer Grace."

Birdie felt the tension seep out of her body, and she collapsed against Gabriel.

"Birdie. My heart nearly stopped when I saw you in there." He drew in a ragged breath. "I have to help put out the fire. Take her away, Higgins. Stay clear. If something happens to her, Higgins, I'll make you personally responsible."

The old man swallowed nervously, then clamped his claw of a hand around Birdie's arm. "Come with me, Your Grace."

Birdie let him take her to the library. She pushed the curtains aside so she could watch the men put out the fire. Her head ached and her throat was raw from the smoke.

Where had all those men been previously? Birdie wondered. Where had they come from? The village had been empty. Now they all gathered in the courtyard, passing buckets of water under Gabriel's orders. Many of them saw him for the first time. Even some women helped. They threw him odd, mistrusting glances, but did not question his authority here.

They put out the fire; however, the building was not salvaged. It burned out entirely; the roof collapsed, and the fragile structure gaped at them sadly with black, empty windows and doors.

Birdie saw Eilidh in the crowd and gestured to her. She came after a moment of hesitation.

"Your Grace." She avoided her eyes.

"Eilidh."

She struggled visibly. Then she met Birdie's eyes. "Thank you for saving my son's life. We were told to stay away from the castle. Now we know why."

"Are you saying someone set fire to the building on purpose?"

Eilidh nodded.

"But why? Why would someone do this? It's meant to be for the children." Birdie felt a helpless rage well up in her.

"You have to find and punish whoever did this."

Birdie walked up and down the library, wringing her hands. "Yes. But who? Who'd do something so despicable?"

"I don't know. I'm so sorry, ma'am," Eilidh whispered.

"I'm sorry too. We will find another room to teach the

children," Birdie told Eilidh. "The main thing is that no one got hurt."

Eilidh's eyes looked troubled. She went to the door, but before she left, said, "I will return to the castle, and Ally will, too. I think Mrs Gowan also intends to return. But the others won't."

"Won't you tell me why?"

Eilidh shook her head. "It is not for me to say. There has always been bad blood between the village people and the old duke. Some men object to it."

That was what Higgins had said earlier as well. "Thank you, Eilidh," Birdie said, utterly exhausted by the day's events.

Birdie took a long bath and scrubbed the smoke out of her skin. Miraculously, she had not a single scar on her body. She dressed in a warm woollen dress. Her throat was still sore, and she drank the elm tea that Cook had sent up.

They had indeed returned, the servants. Birdie frowned. Where was Gabriel? He'd worked as hard as any of the other men earlier. She'd seen him, with rolled-up shirtsleeves, drag crates and barrels out of the adjoining buildings. He'd looked like any of them.

Someone scratched at the door. "His Grace wants to talk to you in the drawing room," Higgins announced after he entered.

"Thank you, Higgins." Birdie ran light-footed up the stairs to the drawing room, where Gabriel was waiting for her.

CHAPTER 18

abriel leaned with one arm against the fireplace as he stared into the fire.

He, too, had taken a bath, and his hair was still damp. He wore a dark-blue coat and breeches and looked every inch a duke. Pride swelled in her. Despite his protestations of not caring, when there was need, when there was an emergency, he'd stepped in like the leader he was, without hesitation. As she always knew he would.

"You won't believe it, Gabriel," she said as she rushed up to him, "but I do believe the villagers are plotting against us. Did you notice that there were no servants at all earlier in the morning? That is, aside from Eilidh, Ally, and the cook. I thought at first it was your terrible reputation as the castle beast, scaring everyone away."

Gabriel looked at her, a serious expression in his eyes. He was not smiling.

"I was joking, of course." She lifted his hand and kissed it. "It is a terrible joke, Gabriel. You know I love you dearly and wouldn't want you looking any other way?" She smiled.

He recoiled as if she'd hit him.

"Gabriel?"

He took her face in his hands. She lifted her mouth for a kiss, but he merely looked down on her. "You are not hurt, are you?" he asked abruptly.

"No. Not a scratch."

"When I saw the fire, I believed you were in the building." His voice shook.

"I know. Poor man. But I was in the village when the fire started."

"Why did you go down to the village?"

"To look for the children. As I said before, no one was here this morning. Didn't you notice? It was so very odd. What is the matter, Gabe?" He was behaving in an odd, aloof manner.

He let go of her hands and paced. "Someone set fire to the school. It wasn't an accident."

"I can't think why anyone would do such a cruel, senseless thing."

"Sit down, Birdie." He led her to the sofa. She sat down and looked up into his serious face. "The fire was an attack against the Duke of Dunross."

Birdie looked at him sceptically. "Do you think so? But who would do such a terrible thing? And why?"

"The people here have little love for the Dukes of Dunross. The old duke wasn't a good man. He chased people off their land so he could turn it into pastures for sheep. He burned down their houses. People are naturally wary of being connected with me, or you, or anyone up here. Even if you mean well."

"Gabriel! That is positively awful. I've heard of the clearances, and it is terrible. But that was the old duke. You are the new duke. You can change things. It is in your power to do so. I would go as far as to say that it is your *duty* to do so."

"The entire place is in more debt than you can possibly

imagine. There is nothing I can do." Gabriel dragged his hands through his thick hair. "There is not much point to it, either."

"There is nothing you can do? Or is there nothing you want to do?"

"This entire discussion isn't about me, but you. Birdie." He was pacing in front of her, and Birdie had the impression that with each step he took, he was transforming more and more into a stranger. "You cannot eradicate century-old hostility by inviting their children to a new school. Especially if the teacher is the duchess herself. Has it ever occurred to you that this attack was specifically targeted against you? It was a warning. The next time, they will target you directly. You will get hurt." He drew in a shaky breath.

Birdie shook her head. "I won't believe it. I can't. What offence can someone take to having someone teach their children? We have set up the school together. The women, themselves, asked me to do it. They helped me. Why burn it all down again?"

Gabriel pulled a hand over his neck. "I don't know, Birdie."

"I believe if one tries hard, one can build connections and eradicate hostility."

He smiled tiredly. "You have wrought miracles in this place, do you know?" He looked around as if only now, for the first time, seeing the dining room. "You have turned a place of dust and stone into proper living quarters." He shook his head with a small smile. "You even set up a bloody school."

"With the help of some women," Birdie said. "Not everyone rejects us."

"Birdie. This can't continue."

"What?" She blinked at him.

"The villagers are no doubt right. The children have no

place up here. The old school needs to be repaired and it will be seen to." He sighed. "They should not come up here to learn."

"But I had the impression you enjoyed it when they were here."

Gabriel shook his head as if that wasn't relevant. "What happened yesterday was a mistake. It should never have happened."

"I am sorry that I did not ask you beforehand about teaching the children in the library."

"I am not talking about the children. I am talking about,"––he lifted a helpless hand––"afterwards." A dull red hue covered his cheeks.

He was not simply referring to the children. He was referring to them. She felt the blood drain from her face.

"No," she whispered.

"Don't you understand?" The words tore from his mouth. "Everything! This infernal responsibility. Now the fire. You. You deserve so much better. I am too bloody damaged for this. I am a broken man. I will drag you down into my personal hell. I've already done so. I have no right to do this. No right at all. I should never have told you all this. Now you are in danger—" He choked. Then he stood up with determination, a hard look in his eye. "I can't be the person you expect me to be. I am sorry."

With that, he walked out of the room.

Birdie remained sitting in her chair, frozen, feeling like she had entered her very own Waterloo.

AFTER WHAT FELT like hours of endless crying, Birdie got up, dried her eyes, and concluded that Gabriel simply didn't love her. He didn't want her. There was nothing to be done. No amount of crying was going to change that fact.

Why should that be such a surprise? It was a discovery that fit neatly into everything else that life had taught her so far. She'd tried, throughout her entire life, to earn other people's affection. Starting from her family, her parents, her siblings, her teachers, yes, even her friends. She'd attempted to do so by being the perfect daughter, the perfect pupil, the perfect friend. Even now—the perfect wife. One who cleaned, cooked, and managed everything. If she tried hard enough, she reasoned, people would like and accept her. She'd sacrificed everything, her own dreams, her own self. For what? For love? For one kind word?

What had she received in return? She'd been taken for granted by all and sundry.

And Gabriel?

She knew in her heart that the man was capable of great loyalty and love. There was a tenderness, kindness, and decency in him that made her heart hammer. The way his eyes lit up unexpectedly when he smiled one of his rare smiles. Or when he looked at her with a wry smile, like he really saw and understood her. With Gabriel, she felt she could be herself. Ironic, given that he believed her to be someone else entirely.

She'd grasped the opportunity to marry Gabriel with both hands. Yet the entire situation was based on deception. The biggest deception, however, had been towards herself. She'd begun the same game she'd played before: if she tried hard enough, he would see value in her and love her.

Well, things didn't work like that. Love didn't work like that. She wasn't about to beg or grovel for his love. She could not fix whatever was broken in him.

It was not her responsibility to do that.

With sudden clarity she realised that, maybe, it had never

been her responsibility to fix anyone in her life: her mother after her father died, her sisters, her brother. Maybe, deep down, she'd believed she was responsible for her father's death. She stared blindly at the dark blue bed curtains.

"I am not," she said out loud. "I was never responsible for any of it."

The hard knot inside her she'd carried around for years loosened. Tears washed it away, and she felt a release.

For the sake of her conscience, she needed to come clean about her deception. She'd tell Gabriel about the real Cecily Burns. Then she'd pack her things and leave.

RESIGNED, Birdie went down to the library. She collected her things with tired movements, placing the books that she'd used to teach the children on a shelf. She picked up a piece of chalk from the floor.

And froze.

Once more, she bent down to the floor.

There it was again. The cold stream of draughty air did not come from the window, for the window was shut and the curtains were drawn. The door was on the left. This cold stream of air came from the other side.

She followed it to the bookshelf. She remembered how, on the first day after her arrival here, she'd felt that there was something odd about this library. She'd found it strange that half of the bookshelf was dusty, almost white with dust, whereas the other half wasn't. When she followed that cold stream of air, it led straight to that ever-clean bookshelf.

Her fingers touched the shelves, tracing the wooden board, the bookends, and found that they felt strange. They weren't leather. She knocked on a book spine. It was wood. An entire row of books consisted of a hard wooden façade of bookends that blended in perfectly with the rest. She pulled on it and heard a mechanism rumble.

The bookshelf slid open without a sound.

Birdie held her breath as she looked down a dark passage. She quickly fetched her candle. The musty, cold, wet smell that wafted up told her that this must be the entrance to the dungeons. Common sense told her it would be a better idea to wait until the morning. But Birdie was in a peckish mood and decided that common sense, or her interpretation thereof, had led her exactly nowhere in her life. Neither had her desire for adventure, but she would not philosophise about this. When a girl was in a medieval castle and had the opportunity to explore a dungeon at midnight, alone in a nightgown, with naught but a candle, naturally she had to precisely do that.

She followed the cold stone steps that wound themselves deeper and deeper underground. Where were they leading? What daredevilry egged her on? She followed a path that seemed endless. Soon, she was in a cellar; to the left and right were vaults with further corridors leading into what seemed a labyrinth of dungeons, but the main stairs twisted further down. Perhaps they led to a torture chamber or oubliette. There would be a dead-end eventually, with maybe a skeleton. Or two.

Her hands reached out to touch the wet stone walls for support as she stepped down. There was a familiar smell in the air. How can it be, Birdie wondered, that I smell the sea? She imagined that she even heard water lapping, but how was that possible? She was inside a building.

She slipped on the stairs, fell, grappled herself upwards, and clung to the slippery wall as she edged her way down. She saw a vague glimmer of light on the bottom.

Her curiosity grew.

She heard voices. Thumping and scraping. Footsteps. The

same sounds she'd heard the first two nights in the castle, and then never again.

Birdie gasped when she realised she found herself not in the dungeons, but in a cave of some sort, filled with crates, boxes, and barrels. The ocean water lapped against the shallow shore, and boats were docked on what appeared to be a tiny indoor harbour. Was this still in the castle? Or were they outside?

Birdie suppressed another gasp when she saw figures moving; she recognised them as the men from the village. They lugged barrels and crates, which they stacked up along the cave wall. One group of men unloaded goods, another took them and carried them out of the cave along a narrow path that led up to the cliffs.

"It was much easier when we could just carry 'em up through the passage, through the hall, and store 'em in the outhouses like we used to," grumbled one man. "Then the lassie arrived and ruined all our plans. Now we have to unload them, upload them on another boat, row to another harbour, unload again. The work is threefold."

"Aye. But after she nearly caught us, it ain't safe."

"The old man kens anyway and ne'er said a peep."

The man dropped the barrel and wiped his forehead. "Aye he knows, and he don't care, specially not with the whisky we give him. But the duke doesnae know."

"The duke's harmless. He doesnae give a tuppence 'bout any of us." The man set down a barrel with a groan and wiped his forehead. "I say, as long as he lets us in peace, we let him in peace."

"Aye but e's no fool, the duke. Logan shouldn't have set the fire. Made the duke suspicious. Stupid thing to do anyhow. Near burnt his own bairn."

Birdie gasped. Logan set the fire! Tommy's father? Why

on earth? She took an involuntary step back and stumbled against one crate.

The men froze immediately.

"Weel, weel, weel. What do we have 'ere?" She whirled around, just in time for her to hear a clank. And then everything went dark.

GABRIEL FELT PHYSICALLY ill when he saw the broken look in Birdie's eyes. It was for the best; he told himself. It was better this way. But then, why did his heart ache when he'd heard her moan as he left the room?

"She's better off this way," he muttered as he paced. He tried to convince himself he was even doing her a favour.

The truth was, he'd felt a rush of icy terror when he'd seen the flames licking into the sky. When he'd realised she was inside the burning building, he had been certain he'd lost her. He hadn't thought twice before charging after her and pulling her out of the inferno. Sudden realisation slammed into his gut. He'd go to hell and back to save her. He couldn't bear it if something ever happened to her, if but one hair on her body got hurt. Earlier, she'd looked up at him with that gentle light in her eyes; she'd said she loved him and wouldn't have him any other way, scars and all. The mere memory of her words caused sweat to break out on his forehead. He hadn't felt nearly as terrified when he faced Napoleon's entire artillery battery in all his wars combined. He'd felt an iron mantle of responsibility close over his shoulders, followed by the sick feeling of certainty that he'd doomed her. Because she loved *him*, he would end up hurting her. The irony, of course, was that to avoid causing her pain, he'd already done so. He wiped his brow with a shaky hand.

He left the room, not even knowing where his feet were leading him. He needed to make sure she was well.

She was not in the drawing room, and her room was empty. Her things were only half packed. He felt relief. Had she gone down to the village again?

He went to the library and stopped short. Birdie was not there, but the bookshelf was open. He stared at it, surprised. He'd heard about secret corridors in castles, so maybe it shouldn't surprise him that there were some in Dunross castle as well. He peeked down the narrow stone stairs.

Birdie, of course, would've gone down all on her own. He swore under his breath.

As he descended the stairs, a sense of foreboding overcame him, of the kind he always felt shortly before the enemy attacked. Odd voices and sounds emerged from below. Blast it. He didn't have his pistol. He crept between a stack of crates and the rock wall.

It looked like all the men from the village were here, lugging crates and barrels. Gabriel was shocked when he saw the reverend, McAloy, heave a sack from a skiff.

Fury rushed through him. If he'd only paid closer attention, he'd have seen the signs. How long had the old duke been dead? Five years. He hadn't arrived here until last year. He'd been too walled up in his tower room to even notice what was going on right beneath this nose. Then Birdie had come prowling around the castle at night. Poking her nose everywhere. Refurnishing rooms—including the outer building.

The fire. Of course. It all came together.

The fire was meant to warn her away.

The entire village was complicit in smuggling, and Dunross castle was their smuggler's den.

CHAPTER 19

a group of village men unloaded the boats and rowed them back to a large ship, which was docked outside somewhere behind a rock. Gabriel ducked lower behind a stack of crates, hoping they wouldn't discover him.

"We could ransom 'er," a burly man said after he dumped a heavy crate down. Given the way the other men acted in his presence, he appeared to be the leader of the group. He had an auburn beard and a cruel look in his eyes.

"I dunno, McKenna. We should leave 'er out of it. She's been a good lass," replied McAloy. The reverend looked troubled.

A bundle on the floor groaned. Gabriel strained his eyes, trying to make out the shape. With horror, he realised the bundle was not a sack, but a person.

It was Birdie! Gabriel shot out of his hiding place with a roar. "What have you done to her, you scum?"

"Weel, weel, weel." McKenna pointed a pistol at him. "The Beast of Dunross in person." He curtseyed in mock obeisance. "How dee do, Yer Grace. I must say I imagined ye a lot more terrifying than ye are." He pointed the gun at Birdie. "Stay where ye are or she dies."

Gabriel froze.

"McKenna. Leave them out of it. I beg ye." McAloy tried to lower his arm. "No good ever comes out of messing with the lairds. Smuggling is one thing. We need it for survival and for feeding our families. It's not as though any of us really enjoy doing it—except for ye. But murder is another matter. Ye'll damn yer soul and get us all hanged."

McKenna pushed him out of the way as he strode towards Gabriel. "I'm done payin' obeisance to the lairds," he spat out. "What good have they ever done to us? They've only brought us death, destruction and despair. Have ye already forgotten?" He looked around wildly at the men who'd dropped their loads and were gaping at Gabriel. Some of them grumbled and nodded.

"Burnt the land. The farms. Drove us away. Took the land for sheep. Aye, and where are they now, the sheep? How are we to survive, I ask ye, Yer Grace? How are we to feed our bairns?"

Gabriel looked at him helplessly. "You are right. You've been done a great injustice. But leave her out of it. She's entirely innocent and has had only had the best in mind for you and your children."

A man with scraggly black hair nodded. "Aye, I can confirm that. Let the lassie go. She's been good to us."

"No." A wild light flickered in McKenna's eyes. "Did they leave our women out of it? No. They burned our huts. Drove our families away. Ye yersel told me, Bruis, that the woman was in the way, prowling around in the library in the middle of the night and taking the outhouse buildings where we store the loot." He spat on the floor. "Transforming it to a bloody school."

"Aye. But when we agreed earlier to scare her away, that

didnae mean ye should burn down the castle," Bruis grumbled. "It was too much. What if the fire had spread? What if someone had got killed?"

"And so they should," McKenna growled. He turned to Gabriel again with a mocking smile. "An eye for an eye. But wait, ye've already lost one," he snickered.

"McKenna, whisht," the reverend intervened, but McKenna swung out with his arm and smashed him in the face, so he crumpled to the ground. Gabriel rushed forward, but three of the men who were nearest to him jumped at him and brought him down. He threw them off with a roar.

At that moment, Birdie jumped up, grabbed a paddle that lay on the floor, and swung it into McKenna's face. But he saw the blow coming and jumped back, firing his pistol, narrowly missing her.

Birdie tripped backwards over a pile of rope, still holding the paddle, and crashed against a stack of crates, which toppled over and knocked out a red-bearded man. She scrambled up again, clutching the paddle.

McKenna narrowed his eyes, reloaded the pistol, and aimed it right at her.

"Move aside Bruis, I have her."

"McKenna. Wait—"

A shot rang out.

Birdie crumpled to the ground.

GABRIEL ROARED. He threw the men off and rushed over to her, swinging his fists. The remaining men hesitated and did not attempt to keep him back. Some pulled their hats.

"McKenna. Now ye've done it," whispered one man as he stared at Gabriel in terrified awe.

His wife lay crumpled over a pile of rope, the paddle across her breast.

Her face was white.

He lifted her and buried his face in her chest, sobbing. He'd always known it would come to that. There really was no point in living any more.

A soft hand buried itself in his hair.

"I'm all right, Gabriel," he heard her spirit whisper. "I feel no pain."

He cried even harder.

The grip in his hair tightened. "Gabriel. I said I am fine." The hand shook his shoulder. "Oof. You're squishing me." She pushed him back.

Her eyes were open and looked at him, full of concern.

"Birdie!" He gasped. "You are not shot? You are not hurt?"

"I merely stumbled over the pile of rope here and hit my head." Birdie winced. "I have *two* bumps now. One from when they discovered me and now this." She looked up. "I don't think McKenna fired that shot. Look."

The men stood in awe around a gaunt, but terrifying, figure who pointed his pistol of Waterloo at them.

"No one touches the Duke of Dunross. Not on my watch," the figure snarled and bared his yellowed teeth. "I'm a better shot than any of you, including His Grace, and he was in the Light Company. Mark you, I can shoot blind, and my bullet will find your heart. And anyone who moves but a hair on his head will get a bullet in his brain."

Higgins.

At his feet, McKenna lay dead.

CHAPTER 20

"*A*re you hurt?" Gabriel checked Birdie's head, her shoulders, her arms.

"I am fine." She scrambled up to her feet. "I only bumped my head."

Higgins stood in front of them, pointing the pistol at the crowd of men. "Stay back. Don't get too close to Their Graces, unless you want to be the next one with a bullet in your heart." The men backed off, lifting their hands in surrender.

"They mean no harm," the reverend said. He had recovered consciousness and had scrambled up. "Please. No more shooting." He moved forward slowly, hands raised, to Logan's crumpled form. He checked Logan's body and confirmed that he was dead, indeed.

Bruis pulled off his hat. "It never should've come to this. We figured a wee bit 'o smugglin' hurts no soul. Needed to feed our families. Wasnae goin' to get rich off it. McKenna here always took things mightily seriously. Was always a bit too passionate, too violent, an' all that. An' now he paid wi his life." He shook his head sorrowfully.

Higgins shuffled over to Gabriel and handed him the pistol. "This is yours, Your Grace. She gave it to me for safe-guarding."

Birdie looked at him apologetically. "I couldn't just leave it in your room like that. Maybe I over-reacted. But after what happened to my father... I thought it better for Higgins to keep."

Gabriel looked at her, shocked, as the implications of her words dawned on him. "Did you think I'd shoot myself? Did I give the impression that I was that far gone?"

She wrung the corner of her shawl in her hands. "Honestly? Yes."

Gabriel shook his head, dazed. "I never would have ... I never thought—" he groped for words.

"I'm sorry. I should've trusted you more," Birdie whispered.

Bruis cleared his throat loudly. "So ... what happens now?"

The men shuffled their feet as they stood around them.

All eyes turned to Gabriel.

He felt the weight of leadership fall on his shoulders. It was a familiar feeling.

He felt the cold metal of the pistol in his hands and closed his eyes for one moment.

Then he nodded as he resigned himself to his fate.

"Bring the stuff up," he ordered.

McKenna's body was laid to rest in the chapel, and a dry-eyed Eilidh kept watch over it. Birdie had told her she'd always have a job here at the castle, and that she and her children would be taken care of. She made a mental note to talk to Higgins about her.

Eilidh had nodded. "You are a good woman, Your Grace," she'd replied.

The men had brought the cargo up to the library.

It really was quite absurd, Birdie reflected, as she saw the men sitting around the massive oaken table in the corridor, talking earnestly with Gabriel.

When had the smuggling adventure turned into a tea party?

Mrs Gowan had arrived with a basket full of freshly baked raisin buns and made tea for everyone. The men had pulled out their flasks of whisky and tipped it into their teacup, slurping loudly as they discussed the events of the day.

Gabriel sat, arms crossed, at the head of the table, and listened silently as they told him about their past and present woes. The past duke had not only neglected his estate and tenants but also confiscated their fields and evicted them from their farms. His intent had been to turn the farmland to pastures for sheep, because sheep's wool brought in more profit than agriculture. But he'd never bought the sheep. In the absence of any true leadership after the old duke's death, the villagers had turned to smuggling to maintain their livelihood. Yet Gabriel had been oblivious to all this. Deeply immersed in his own problems, he'd not bothered to learn about the people's welfare. By the time he'd arrived at the castle, they'd been smuggling for several years already, under Logan's leadership. They'd been importing brandy, rum, and tea, and exported illegally produced whisky.

The "ghost", the white sheet that Birdie had discovered on the barbican, had been their way of communicating. They hadn't counted on the duke bringing in a new duchess, especially not one who stuck her nose into every nook and cranny, even at night.

"Every time we put it out, it means the bootleg arrives

that night. Women and children stay put at home. To us men, it means: don't go through the library. Take the outside path to the cave. We knew His Grace would never leave the tower."

Gabriel winced.

"But with Her Grace prowling around at night, it wasn't safe to use the secret passage in the library. And Logan said, if it frightened Her Grace, so much the better. Apologies, Yer Grace," Bruis explained.

"What about McKenna burning down the school?" asked Birdie. She glared at the men. "What was that good for?"

"Aye, that wasn't necessary. McKenna said with all the bairns up here, there was too much traffic. Couldn't do our work properly. Best to keep everyone away. Not that I agreed wi' any of it. He nearly killed his own kid, too." Bruis shook his head.

Higgins had returned to his butler role and was serving the men. They looked at him with respect.

"What about you, Higgins? Did you know about any of this?" Gabriel looked at him sternly.

"Of course, Your Grace." He served tea with a serenity that astounded Gabriel.

"And it never occurred to you to tell me about it?"

"No, Your Grace, I didn't think it'd interest you."

Gabriel searched for words. Maybe there was a grain of truth in Higgins' words. But now, he could no longer pretend to be disinterested. His library was full of bootlegged whisky and other contraband. The people looked to him for leadership.

After everyone had left, Birdie hesitated. Gabriel remained sitting at the table, deep in thought. "So many people wanting something from you," she said with a wan smile. "You will be very busy fixing everyone's lives."

Gabriel looked up, startled. "Birdie. I didn't know you were still here."

She felt a pang. It reminded her of her own predicament; that her position here was anything but secure. She sat down in the empty chair next to his. It was time for some plain speaking. It was time for him to know the truth.

"I wanted to talk to you about something. Before I leave," she began.

Before she could continue, Gabriel pulled her into his lap and buried his head into her hair. The hairs on her neck stood on end. "For one moment I thought I'd lost you." His voice sounded husky. "I couldn't have borne it."

"Gabriel," Birdie said helplessly. "I need to tell you something."

He lifted his head and frowned. "Is there someone arriving?"

The sound of wheels crunching on the gravel outside heralded the arrival of a coach.

Hurrying footsteps slapped on the stone stairs outside. The brass knocker boomed.

"Coming, coming," Higgins grumbled and made his way towards the door. He swung it open.

"Well. I must say. This is a fine establishment you got yourself here," someone said an all too familiar voice.

A young man, looking from head to toe like a veritable tulip, twirled his walking stick as he looked around curiously.

Birdie gasped. "Freddie!"

Her brother Alfred had arrived.

CHAPTER 21

"*H*ullo old mum. Fancy finding you here." Freddie tapped his stick on the floor. "Bang up place, this. A bit old, no? Does the stone hold or will it come crumbling down on my head?"

Gabriel had scrambled to his feet.

"Ah. You are the Duke of Dunross, I presume?" Freddie took off his hat and made a flourishing obeisance.

"Yes. And you are?" Gabriel looked like the wind had been taken out of his sails.

"Alfred Talbot, Baron of Tottingham at your service. Birdie's brother. Call me Freddie. I say, I like your eyepatch. Your scars, too. All the crack since that Byron fellow. But what is this?" He strolled over to the table and sniffed. His face brightened. "I smell whisky. May I?" He poured himself some of the caramel-coloured liquid into a glass and tasted it.

"I don't understand." Gabriel looked around for Birdie.

"Prime." Freddie lifted the glass, held it against the light, and squinted into it. "You Scots sure know how to brew some powerful stuff. The elixir of life, this is."

"Brother?" Gabriel pressed his fingers against his temple. "I was not aware you had a brother."

"And two bloody sisters, spinsters both, and a mother who claims to be an invalid, even though she's healthier than a horse," Freddie added blithely before he took another sip. "And a dog, and a cat," he added in an afterthought. "The parrot died. Thank the stars. But now mum is in mourning over the creature and refuses to leave her room. I say, sis. Been missing you awfully. Heard you got yourself married to a duke. That maid of yours croaked and tried it with blackmail but can't squeeze blunt out of where there ain't any." He flashed a grin and looked so charming in the process that even Birdie understood how her brother wheedled every last penny out of his bankers' vaults.

But Mary! Oh! That faithless, disloyal maid. She must have returned straight away to her family and sought out Freddie to tell on her.

"Since I was feeling the pinch in my pocket, and things were getting tight, I thought it time to whip off and visit my sis up here in the northern wastelands before they box me up. Say, you're my brother-in-law!" Freddie's face brightened as he turned to Gabriel, who took a step back. "That's a bang-up thing, to have a duke as a brother-in-law. Rich and powerful, with castles and all. I daresay you have a mighty influence on certain people. Came to see whether it's true."

"Freddie! Do be quiet." Birdie's eyes filled with tears. She wished she could sink into the ground with shame. Turning to Gabriel, she said, "I wanted to explain. At this very moment. But of course, my infernal brother had to intervene."

"What is it you wanted to explain, Birdie?" Gabriel asked in a deadly quiet tone.

"Dished you up a Banbury tale, my sister dear did." Freddie cheerfully poured himself another glass and was oblivious to his sister's dagger stares. "As did that other girl. Sicily. Sassily. Cecily. Yes. That's it. Cecily."

"Cecily Burns?" Gabriel's face was hewn of granite. He turned to Birdie. "My understanding was that you were Roberta Cecily Burns Talbot. You insisted on signing the parish register that way."

"Only Roberta Talbot." Birdie felt ill. "I tried to tell you just now."

"Swapped places with th' other one." Freddie made a swapping motion with his hands, while still holding his whisky glass. "Very cleverly done. Didn't think you had it in you, old girl. Say, do you also have other types of whisky?" he asked Higgins.

Miraculously, Higgins understood.

"Yes, my Lord. Crates and crates full of them," Higgins muttered. "Brandy too. Freshly smuggled from France."

"I like this place!" Freddie was ecstatic. "What a prime old codger. Show me, man. Lead the way!" He followed Higgins out of the hall.

Gabriel's eyes never left Birdie's face. "You are not Cecily Burns."

"No," Birdie whispered. She couldn't meet his eyes. She felt like the worst scum that existed on the face of this earth. She heard him breathe heavily.

"I have no excuse," she stammered. "I was about to tell you the entire story. I met Cecily in a coach; she was on the way to Scotland. She didn't—oh, Gabriel. I'm so sorry. She didn't want to marry you. She was crying the entire time. I was on the way to my new position as a governess. I was supporting my family." She waved her hand toward Freddie, who'd disappeared with Higgins through the library door, followed by the noise of barrels being wrenched open. "You've got a taste of what they are like," she blurted out. "I was so tired of my life and of having to toil for a family who wasted away our entire fortune. It was no life. I didn't know what to do. Then I met Cecily, and she suggested we trade positions. It was her idea. You must believe me! It wasn't a malicious deception. Yes, it was dishonest and cowardly. But at that time, it seemed like an excellent thing to do; to escape my life by stepping into someone else's. It isn't an excuse at all, I know. But at the time I was so desperate, and I thought it was the best thing that could've happened to me."

"What? To marry a complete stranger who was someone else's bridegroom and to deceive him and lie to him?" Gabriel's voice sounded hard with condemnation.

Her shoulders slumped.

"All this time you've let me believe you are someone else entirely. You've had ample opportunity to come clear, yet you didn't."

Birdie winced. "I know," she whispered. She really had no excuse other than she'd got herself so caught up in this fairy tale that she'd veritably believed it was true. She'd willed herself to forget that it had been a deception. "There is no excuse I can offer."

"When you said that vow in church." Gabriel swallowed as if the words pained him. "You lied even as you said it."

Birdie hung her head.

"You've not only dishonoured your vow. You've dishonoured mine. Twice." Gabriel got up. "I vowed to my father, and to Cecily's, that I'd take care of the girl. You intervened. You made that impossible. Then the marriage vow. You vowed to *love* me." His voice cracked a little on the word "love." "It was nothing but a lie."

Birdie remained in her chair, frozen.

"No, Gabriel, never that, never a lie…"

She heard his footsteps recede as he left the hall.

. . .

BIRDIE DIDN'T WAIT.

She jumped into her brother's carriage and ordered the driver to return from where he came from.

After bribing him with a velvet pouch, the horses galloped over the drawbridge.

She'd give him a second pouch if they drove even faster. A little voice told her she needn't bother, for Gabriel wouldn't come after her.

As the horses galloped over the drawbridge and Dunross Castle disappeared in the distance, Birdie knew, without doubt, that she'd lost him forever.

CHAPTER 22

"There's a young woman here to see you, Madam." Sally, the maid, stood in the doorway awaiting a reply.

Eleonore Hilversham looked up from her papers. She was in her early thirties, but the severity with which she pulled back her fine silver-blonde hair made her look older than she was.

She pursed her lips. "Name?"

"She wouldn't say." Sally was new and did not yet recognise the parents of pupils.

"Send her in, then."

Miss Hilversham jumped out of her chair when a bedraggled figure staggered into the room.

"I didn't know where else to go." Her lips trembled.

"Birdie!" As Miss Hilversham embraced her, the girl burst into noisy sobs.

"There, there." Miss Hilversham patted her head. "Calm yourself. Surely things are not as bad as that?" She gave her a handkerchief, and Birdie blew her nose noisily.

"You're meant to be teaching at the Willowburys. Did

something happen?" She drew Birdie to a chair. Birdie collapsed into it with a sigh.

"So much happened. I scarce know where to begin."

Miss Hilversham sat behind her desk and steepled her fingers. "One best begins at the beginning, child."

And so Birdie told her the entire tale.

After concluding the tale with her retreat from the castle, Birdie fell silent. Miss Hilversham took off her spectacles and rubbed her eyes tiredly. "I am, honestly, at a loss for words. You've always been my most sensible student. How you managed to get yourself into this fix is beyond me. But what is done is done. You've ruined your reputation hopelessly."

Birdie blinked. "Reputation? To be fair, Miss Hilversham, that is the last thing on my mind."

Miss Hilversham sighed. "You married under a false name. Did you think that marriage would be valid?"

"I didn't think," Birdie replied with a shaky voice. "At first, it was an adventure. A gorgeous adventure. And then, you know, I really enjoyed being married. I am *good* at being married. I was good at being a duchess, too. The people started trusting in me. Well, that is, the women and children. The men are a different matter, what with their smuggling and all that. But, Miss Hilversham, I thought I could have a future there. I could bring about change, improve their lives for the better... You must believe me. I completely forgot that it was all based on a deception, a lie. I—" Her shoulders shook, and she brought forth between sobs. "I love him so." She wiped her cheek with the handkerchief. "And he despises me, which he has every right to."

Miss Hilversham looked at her with a worried frown. "You need to rest, child. And then we will have to think about what path remains open to you. If you do not enjoy teaching, you will find little joy teaching at my school."

Birdie smiled a wan smile. "I did not enjoy being a governess, working and living with the genteel families. But I very much enjoyed teaching the little ones from the village. They were unspoiled and hungry for learning and so grateful for everything I offered."

"Yet I am not entirely convinced that teaching is your vocation." Miss Hilversham tapped the tip of her quill on a sheet of paper. "We shall have to see. For now, Sally will show you a room. Go have a long nap."

"Yes, Miss Hilversham." Birdie curtsied, as they had been taught to do as students. Then she impulsively hugged her former teacher. Miss Hilversham patted her back gently.

After Birdie had left, the schoolmistress sighed. Then she stared at the paper in front of her.

With some resolve, she dipped her quill into the inkstand.

To the Duchess of Ashmore, Oxfordshire.

"Dear Duchess. My dearest Lucy…"

IF HE HEARD one more word about whisky, types of whisky, whisky distillation, whisky ageing, and the general history of whisky, he would scream.

Gabriel threw an irritated look at Freddie, who was now waxing poetic on the topic of whisky caskets. The fop had been making himself home in his castle since the moment he'd arrived and showed no sign of leaving. Given the dandy he was, he'd acquired a tiresome amount of knowledge about everything concerning whisky, which he insisted on sharing with Gabriel.

What astounded him even more was that he'd forged a close relationship with Higgins, of all people. The old man fairly doted on the fop. It turned out that Higgins was as much of a whisky lover as he was. That he'd recently point-blank shot a black-hearted scoundrel impressed him even more. Apparently, they were kindred souls.

Gabriel massaged his temples.

Birdie had been gone for a fortnight already, and he hadn't gone after her. He felt helpless, angry, and confused.

The moment they realised she'd gone, Freddie had clapped him on the shoulders and said, "The old girl probably ran all the way home. Give her time, she'll come around. Trust me, I know my sister." Gabe thought that maybe there was a word of wisdom in there.

Freddie was dressed in a pink waistcoat and striped, yellow pantaloons. His waist was cinched, the shoulders padded, the coat sleeves puffed. Gabriel guessed he must wear a corset. The starched shirt points nearly poked him into his cheeks. His pale blonde hair was elegantly styled and protruded over his forehead in an elaborate wave. He seemed like a veritable pink of the fashion, but Gabriel couldn't say for sure, since he hadn't been in society the last seven years. Possibly longer.

"I say. Did you hear at all what I was saying?"

Gabriel jerked to attention. "Something about grains."

"These barrels of barley beg to be put to good use! It would be a crime not to!"

"Where on earth have you acquired all this knowledge?"

Freddie smirked. "You wouldn't believe the kinds of people one meets in the gaming halls of London. Oh, the information they are willing to share!"

Ah.

"So, you are a gambler. Instead of helping your mother and sisters, you're gambling their dowries away." Gabriel wasn't born yesterday; he'd put two and two together. A baron's daughter who became a governess only did so if she found herself in strained circumstances.

He eyed Freddie's clothes critically. Nothing about the

way he dressed implied he was in dire straits. He thought of the state of Birdie's clothes. Simple. Plain. Obviously refashioned from old gowns. Not that he knew too much about it. She certainly didn't parade about in the finest of silks and velvets. No. She said she had to work as a governess ... to pay Freddie's gaming debts?

His knuckles tightened. What about the sisters? He suddenly had a vision of them garbed in the finest gowns in London.

"Dowries? No. My father did that. Shortly before he gave the crows a pudding."

Gabriel looked at him blankly. "I beg your pardon?"

"Dropped his leaf? Kicked the bucket?" He folded down three fingers in imitation of a pistol and tipped the forefinger against his temple.

Gabriel uttered an oath.

"Before that, he gambled away our entire fortune and estate, save the house in which we now live." Freddie shrugged. "Been trying to gamble it all back. Alas, Lady Fortuna hasn't been in a cooperative mood lately."

"Gambling would not rectify your situation in any manner. It would only make it worse."

"What else am I to do? It's the only thing I'm good at. Say, do you play?" Freddie pulled out a pack of cards from his inner coat pocket.

Gabriel warded off with both hands. "No."

"Shame."

"No gambling under my roof. If I catch you as much as playing for a farthing, I'll throw you out."

"No need for a tiff, Your Grace. I won't gamble. I daresay I've lost my taste for it. There are other, better ways of making money."

"Such as making your sister work as a governess."

"That's one way. Turned out to be unreliable because she

ran off and married a duke, see. But I was meaning something else." Freddie lifted his whisky glass to his lips. "We have all the material we need stored in your cellar. Save for a copper still and some piping, which no doubt we can have made by some local."

"Since when has this become 'we'?"

Freddie clapped him on his shoulder. "Of course, it is 'we,' brother-in-law. You and I will brew a whisky like the world had never seen, or rather, tasted before. And we'll grow filthily rich in the process."

"You know that would be illegal."

"Pouf. Illegal. You are a duke. Make it legal." Freddie leaned forward, an eager look on his face. "You have the manpower, don't you? The water from the loch. There's got to be a loch somewhere? They're littered all over Scotland. Need lots of water for whisky."

There was, indeed, Loch Drumdross nearby. Gabriel had an entire village full of eager manpower. His estates were in shambles and needed drastic financial overhaul that his captain's pension would not cover. Gabriel stroked his chin. Maybe the tulip had a point.

"You can chuck out caskets and caskets of whisky. Single malt whisky. Blended malt whisky. Vatted malt whisky. Mind you, it'll take a while, at best three years or longer. But until then you have the lovely, bootlegged booze over there." Freddie patted the whisky bottle lovingly. "And brandy, too What are you going to do with it all? Surely not send it back to the frogs? They don't deserve it. Best is you drink it yourself." Freddie grinned at him so charmingly that Gabriel felt a return smile tugging at the corner of his mouth.

"Very well, Tottingham. It is worth a try. Under one condition: it's going to be legal."

"There's no profit in it if we go legal—" Freddie started, but Gabriel raised his hand.

"That is my condition. Or we forget the entire enterprise."

Freddie grumbled. Then held out his hand. "Deal. Legal. You will take care of the paperwork, and I will take care of the ins and outs of whisky making. You need not worry a thing over it." He cracked his fingers.

"How do I know I can trust you?"

"Of course you can trust me!" Freddie placed a manicured hand over his heart. "You wound me to the quick. A Talbot is eminently trustable. You've married my sis' after all. Not that I blame you."

"Your sister is not here, in case you haven't noticed. She has deceived me rather grossly."

"So she has! Inconceivable, really. One wouldn't have thought that she had it in her."

Gabriel shook his head. "You really are a terrible brother, Freddie."

Freddie grew serious. "I suppose I am. But you know what. Whatever she's done, for whatever motivation, I know one thing. My sister is gold. She's worth three times the likes of me. Maybe four. It pains me to say it, but she's the only sensible person in the family. As good as a man. Better." His face grew grim. "She held everyone together after father bit the grass. Do you know who found him in the study, after he'd done the deed?"

A feeling of horror overcame Gabriel. "No."

"Yes."

Gabriel closed his eyes.

"I may be a wastrel, but I know my sister's worth." Freddie leaned forward. "The question is: do you?"

Freddie suddenly seemed ages older than his youthful self as he stared into Gabriel's eyes.

"I love your sister as I've loved no one ever before," Gabriel said hoarsely.

Freddie quirked his lips into a quick grin. "Prime. That's a bit over the top for my taste, but it'll do. I suppose she'll be back. Unless you decide to fetch her back, which might be the thing to do. 'Til then, there is work to do. I will document everything, every design, and inform you of every move I make. Nothing underhand, I assure you. I will inform Higgins. He will be delighted."

Freddie got up and walked away, whistling a tune to himself. At the bottom of the stairs, he paused and turned.

"Oh, and brother-in-law. Your Grace. Forgive me, but it must be said. If by chance you intend to seek her out personally, which may not be such a terrible idea, I would consider a change of linen. An entire overhaul of Your Grace's wardrobe would be recommended. You look like you emerged directly from the bowels of a pirate ship from the previous century. If advice is needed"––he bowed––"this body will be more than happy to provide it. I tend to be somewhat of a connoisseur of fashion. And whisky," he added, lest Gabriel forgot that crucial piece of information.

With those words, he minced down the servants' stairs in search of Higgins.

Gabriel sighed. Maybe his brother-in-law had a point. It was time for him to leave his tower and re-enter the world.

He had to go after Birdie.

CHAPTER 23

*S*o this is where Birdie spent her childhood, Gabriel mused as the carriage turned onto Paradise Road in Bath. It came to a halt in front of a grey, formidable-looking mansion house with a Palladian portico. On a marble slate was engraved Miss Hilversham's Seminary for Young Ladies.

A peal of girlish laughter rang from the gardens surrounding the house.

Gabriel ducked behind a tree.

Then he straightened his top hat and pulled down his tightly fitting coat. Blast Freddie! He'd ordered the tailor to make it tighter than he normally wore, and now it stretched uncomfortably across his chest and arms. But apparently, it was all the crack, as Freddie had assured him earnestly. The young man had accompanied him to Inverness to make sure he was clothed properly.

"You must have a Weston coat," Freddie had insisted. "And Wellington boots. Is there a Hoby's in Inverness?"

Gabriel had no clue. "Who, or what is Hoby's?" he'd countered testily.

Freddie had nearly had a heart attack. "Hoby's, Your Grace, is London's most esteemed bootmaker," he'd explained after he recovered from the shock. "He makes the best Wellingtons in the entire kingdom. They are made of the finest, softest calfskin leather and are shined to glossy perfection. Don't settle for anything less."

Gabriel had been rather irritated. The last time he checked, Wellington was the name of his field marshal, not of a boot. He knew for a fact that Wellington's boots had been mud and blood splattered. It eluded him entirely why those boots, sensible as they were, had to be this tightly cut, as well as polished to such an extent that he could see his mirror image in them.

But oddly enough, he rather trusted Freddie's sense of fashion more than his own. If it were up to him, Gabriel would've kept on his linen shirt, which sported holes, and his black leather trousers which had grease spots that refused to come out. Blast it, but Freddie was undoubtedly right; he needed to improve his wardrobe.

He'd also had his hair cut in the newest fashion. The hairdresser who, most irksomely, had been French, had insisted that he wear his hair à la Brute. This meant that his hair would be brushed forward, so that it cascaded over his right temple and down his cheek, hiding the ear and semi-covering the burn scars.

"Eet weel look most fetching, seigneur," the toad had said and danced about him with scissors.

"Bah," Gabriel replied, unnerved at the thought that some years ago he may have shot this man's kin without a second thought.

Thus pruned, plucked, primed, polished, and primped, Gabriel stood in front of Miss Hilversham's Seminary for Young Ladies in search of his wife.

The maid who opened the door looked at him cluelessly.

"One moment, sir," she mumbled, and bid him wait in the corridor.

It smelled of paper, wax polish, and a feminine smell that he couldn't quite decipher. Something flowery. Maybe violets.

A tall, slender woman quietly descended the stairs. She looked ageless with silver hair and silver eyes and looked at him inquiringly in a straightforward, regal manner. This, no doubt, must be Miss Hilversham.

Gabriel gulped. "Ma'am." He took off his hat.

"The Duke of Dunross, I presume." Her voice was cool and clear.

He was taken aback. "How did you know that?"

"If you would follow me, Your Grace." She turned without answering his question.

Gabriel followed her, feeling his nervousness rise.

They walked down a corridor, with doors to his left and right.

One door was open, and he saw oaken tables, a blackboard, and shelves stuffed with books. Girls in similar pale blue dresses bent their heads over the books. A silent hush told him they were studying.

"It is quite extraordinary," said Gabriel. "A girl's school like this, I mean. It isn't too common." Blast it. That woman made him nervous, but one had to say something.

The woman threw him an assessing look. "No, it isn't too common. This is the best academy in the country. If you will have a seat, Your Grace." She pointed at a chair that stood in front of a rather large writing table. He sat down and felt rather small.

"Miss Talbot studied here for several years. She was one of my best and brightest students."

Gabriel sat up proudly. "Of course, she'd be."

"We teach the girls more than just the belle arts.

Languages, History, Natural Sciences. Geography, and Advanced mathematics."

"That is an impressive list." Certainly more than he'd ever learned.

"The school has currently less than twenty students. I like to keep the numbers low, though some may say twenty is large enough." Miss Hilversham picked up a quill and pulled it between her fingers. "I hire the best teachers in the country. None but the best will do for my girls."

"Naturally." He did not know where this conversation was going.

"Excellent education like we provide here requires a considerable number of resources, such as a lapidarium where the girls may study at their own pace."

"Naturally." Gabriel was out of his depth and did not know what a lapidarium was.

Miss Hilversham steepled her fingers and lifted a narrow eyebrow. "A lapidarium, Your Grace, is a type of museum that exhibits stone sculptures, artworks and artefacts. Lapidarium, coming from the Latin lapis, meaning stone, refers to such a collection. It would be highly beneficial for the girls to have their own lapidarium, particularly since our garden seems to harbour some Celtic and Roman artefacts that are worthwhile to exhibit. Artefacts which one, naturally, would exhibit in a lapidarium."

"Oh. I see! You do not have this lapidarium yet."

"No, Your Grace, we do not."

"But you would like to have one."

"Yes, Your Grace, we very much would like to." Her voice was deceptively soft.

"And you need funding."

"It is a coarse term. Shall we call it patronage? The school has been tremendously lucky to have two dukes who are patrons of this school; one more so than the other, and if one is honest, it is the duchesses who are the patronesses, not the dukes. It would be very beneficial to have a third. A school that can boast three dukes as patrons would be quite exceptional."

"Naturally," Gabriel said automatically. "I will be more than happy to be this third patron."

Miss Hilversham actually smiled. It took him aback because, with this smile, her entire being transformed; there was an inkling of a rather attractive woman behind the severe façade. "I see we understand each other, Your Grace. Now. Regarding Birdie."

Gabriel leaned forward eagerly. "Yes? Can I talk to her?"

"May I ask what your intentions are towards the girl?"

He frowned. "She is my wife. There needs to be nothing more added."

"Is she, indeed?"

He bristled. "We were married in a ceremony in Scotland. There were witnesses."

"Gathering from Birdie's description, the reverend married her under the wrong name, even though she signed the register under her own. I believe the marriage to be invalid. Particularly since you were led to believe, until fairly recently, that she was an entirely different person."

Gabriel stared at her. Dash it, the woman was right.

He ran both hands through his carefully coiffed Brutus mane, destroying it entirely.

"So, you see, you have no obligation towards Birdie at all," the woman continued. "You may not even need to annul the marriage since it was never valid to begin with."

Gabriel sat up, stung. "I am not interested in annulment. As far as I'm concerned, she is my wife, and it is my duty to care for her."

"Duty?" Miss Hilversham threw him a shrewd look. "Is she a mere *duty* to you now?"

"With all due respect, madam. This is none of your concern. But if you must know, I care deeply for her." He drew a shaky breath. "I cannot imagine a life without her."

"And it took you over a month to realise that?"

He felt himself blush.

Her steely look held his gaze one moment longer. Then she gave a curt nod. "Very well, Your Grace—"

A knock on the door interrupted her. A girl with two thick auburn braids entered and curtsied quickly. "Beg your pardon, Miss Hilversham. I was just meaning to ask whether we may go out in the garden now that we finished the assignment." She looked at Gabriel. "Oh! Your face!" she blurted out.

"Katherine Merivale, where are your manners? This is no way to greet our guests," Miss Hilversham's voice cut through the atmosphere in the room.

The girl coloured and stammered. "I beg your pardon, I didn't mean—"

"Merivale?" interrupted Gabriel. "Did you say Merivale?"

The girl curtsied. "Yes, sir. I beg your pardon. My name is Katy Merivale."

Gabriel gripped the side of his chair that his knuckles whitened. "Are you, by any chance, acquainted with a Philip Merivale?"

"Yes sir. He is my father."

Gabe breathed heavily. "You mean to say he *was* your father as he—he fell in battle? At Waterloo?"

Katy threw him a curious glance. "No sir. He is very much alive."

"It can't be." Gabriel felt the blood leave his face.

"You may go now, Katy," said Miss Hilversham, "and yes take the girls outside in the fresh air for half an hour."

"Yes, Miss Hilversham." The girl curtsied and threw a last curious look at Gabriel before she left.

Miss Hilversham played with her quill. "What do you intend to do, Your Grace?"

Gabriel still couldn't wrap his head around the fact that Merivale might be alive. It was a mistake. It was a different Merivale. But first, Birdie. Birdie was what mattered. He'd go down on his knees and beg if he had to.

"I need to find Birdie. Please, Miss Hilversham. Help me."

The teacher nodded. "You are in luck and will be able to catch two birds with one stone. I sent Miss Talbot to the Ashmore residence in Oxfordshire a fortnight ago. You will find her there."

Gabriel had no idea what she was talking about, killing two birds with one stone, but he shook her hand gratefully.

CHAPTER 24

*B*irdie was reading *The Romance of the Forest* to the Dowager Duchess Augusta Ashmore, who sat in a dark blue winged chair and snored so loudly she woke Bart, the three-legged dog, who napped by her feet. Birdie was well aware she'd lost her listener; however, she continued reading. There was something soothing about reading words out loud. At least she didn't have to think whilst she spoke. Or talk to her friends Lucy and Arabella, who were sitting on a sofa nearby, drinking tea, and conversing with hushed voices.

Birdie loved her friends dearly. But right now, she could not bear their concerned glances and worried frowns they gave her every time she was in their presence.

Lucy, the Duchess of Ashmore, was a lively thing with a head full of brown, unruly curls. Her mouth never stopped moving. She was married to a man completely her opposite, the powerful and, Birdie thought, rather frightful Duke of Ashmore who rarely smiled. She did not know what Lucy saw in him, but the two seemed to be one heart and one soul. The man melted every time he was in Lucy's presence. Lucy herself transformed into a bundle of bliss every time he was around.

Birdie sighed. Gabriel had never seemed to melt in that manner when she was nearby. The only influence she'd had on the man was that he'd had a tendency to run away and lock himself up in a tower.

So much for him loving her.

She sighed again.

Arabella was the duke's sister and therefore Lucy's sister-in-law. Her strawberry blonde hair was coiffed back neatly and her aristocratic nose and forehead left no doubt as to whose family she belonged to. Arabella had always been the gentle, sweet one in their group of friends. Yet she'd proven to have a stubbornness and thirst for adventure that equalled Lucy's.

She, too, had married for love. Philip Merivale, the Duke of Morley, was more of an engineer than a duke. Birdie had merely blinked when, at their introduction, he'd shot the question at her about whether she agreed that the new steam propulsion technology was already outdated before it had become fashionable.

"For travelling by air is the new future, madam. Would you agree?" he'd asked.

"Er——"

"I take that as a yes." He'd beamed at her, then whirled off to convince Ashmore to install an automated platform in Ashmore Hall that would vertically transport not only freight but also people. Ashmore had listened, interested.

Watching her friends together with their husbands and families, Birdie was conscious of a painful pang in her heart. She was an outsider. An invisible bubble of bliss and contentment surrounded them.

She felt she was like a black blemish in the middle of a colourful spring meadow.

Birdie shifted uncomfortably.

"Birdie, dear, I daresay you can stop reading now that grandmamma is deeply asleep. She will be quite upset to miss all you've read while she slept and no doubt will make you re-read it all later on," Arabella said in her gentle voice.

Birdie shut the book and pushed up her spectacles.

Lucy threw her a measured look. Birdie fidgeted. Speaking from experience, it never boded well when Lucy had that look in her eyes.

"Let's take a walk in the park." Lucy took her firmly by the arm and raised her to her feet.

"I should probably get changed…" Birdie murmured.

"Nonsense. Supper is in three hours. The children are busy, and the men are concocting whatever next improvement of Ashmore Hall. Grandmamma will sleep until supper. Gives us ample time to take a walk, the three of us. Alone."

Arabella nodded and took Birdie's other arm.

The three stepped out onto the veranda and walked towards the generous lake that graced the park of Ashmore Hall. It really was magnificent, even in autumn.

"I have a plan," Lucy said, getting straight to the point.

"Oh no. I knew you were up to something." Birdie groaned. "We always get into trouble every time you have a plan."

"Pray tell, Lucy. You always come up with the best things." Arabella had absolute faith in Lucy's machinations.

"When I received Miss Hilversham's letter about you, begging me to take you in—which, by the by, is the most ridiculous thing I ever received––you know I need no one's letter to take any of my friends in? Not even Miss Hilversham's, and you know how I love the woman to bits."

Birdie nodded, a knot in her throat.

"So, as I was saying. Miss Hilversham merely confirmed

that you were up to something. Arabella and I knew long ago that you were going to get yourself into trouble, didn't we?"

Arabella nodded. "Oh, yes."

"But how?"

"You sent that letter from Inverness if you recall."

Birdie stared at her. Then slapped her forehead. "I did, didn't I! I had forgotten about it."

"It sounded ominous, like a goodbye letter, like you didn't expect to see us again, you goose." Lucy elbowed her.

"I wrote it in the last inn before going north. I daresay I felt rather uneasy about swapping with Cecily."

Birdie had, of course, told her friends everything as soon as she'd arrived at Ashmore Hall.

"As I was saying, when I received Miss Hilversham's letter, I knew you'd fallen in love."

Birdie protested.

"No arguing. It is plain for everyone to see, isn't it, Arabella?"

Arabella threw Birdie a sympathetic look and nodded. "You are suffering the pangs of love rather dreadfully, dear friend."

Birdie felt a flush creep up her neck.

"So this man, this captain—"

"He's a duke," Birdie interrupted.

Lucy and Arabella exchanged glances. "Three friends, three dukes, and one wishing well. I say no more. I wonder when the fourth shows up? But I veer off-topic."

Birdie merely looked at her, bewildered. "What are you saying?"

Lucy waved a hand. "No matter. We will never finish this conversation at this rate. Let me speak and you listen."

"You certainly have become bossy since becoming a duchess," Birdie grumbled.

"This duke you love," Lucy said, and Birdie cringed. "He is

in that castle in Scotland. He won't forgive a girl's prank and hasn't written, or shown himself since you've left since when?"

"Over a month ago." Birdie hung her head.

"Confound the man. This is no way to go about winning his true love's heart." Lucy frowned.

"But Lucy. This is precisely the point. Don't you see? He doesn't love me!" Birdie had no more tears left, but saying the words tugged at her heart. "It's the opposite. He positively despises me. After all I've done to him."

"After all you've done? Hm. Let me see." Lucy ticked off her fingers. "Got his house in order. Hired retainers. Opened a modern village school. Uprooted a nest of smugglers."

"That was Higgins, really, not me," Birdie countered.

"I positively must meet this Higgins," Lucy raved.

"You must not. He's senile and quite deaf."

"And he shoots like the devil. What a brilliant man." Lucy would not be deterred from the notion that Higgins was the best butler who ever existed in the entire kingdom.

"Anyway, Lucy, what was your plan?" asked Arabella.

"My plan is this," she replied. The three friends huddled closely together, exactly as they used to at the seminary, whenever Lucy concocted some particular pernicious prank. "When Mahomet does not come to the mountain, then the mountain must go to Mahomet."

"Lucy." Birdie took off her spectacles and rubbed her nose tiredly. "You're not making any sense whatsoever."

"Badger the man out of his tower. Storm his defences. Make him see reason. Speak the only language he understands, the military one. It is the only way." Lucy set her chin stubbornly.

Birdie shook her head. "No Lucy. Out of the question. I will not return to him."

"You need not fear. Arabella and I are coming with you."

Arabella blinked. "Are we?"

Lucy nodded. "Between the three of us, he will relent."

Birdie didn't know whether to laugh or cry.

A footman came huffing across the lawn.

Lucy squinted at him. "Felix? Is anything the matter?"

"Yes, Your Grace. I mean, no, Your Grace." He took a big breath. "You must forgive me, Your Graces. One tends to get somewhat confused. But Your Grace's presence is required. It appears His Grace has arrived."

"Felix. Whatever on earth are you talking about?"

He gestured helplessly. "His Grace."

"Yes, we know." Lucy sighed. "There are two of them, in fact. The Duke of Ashmore, and the Duke of Morley."

"I beg your pardon, Your Grace, I was meaning his Grace, the Duke of Dunross."

Birdie nearly toppled into the pond. Lucy grabbed her in time to pull her back. "It can't be," Birdie whispered.

Lucy clapped her hands, delighted. "See, Birdie? The mountain need not move after all."

They entered the drawing room the moment the butler announced the Duke of Dunross.

It was unmistakeably Gabriel.

He held his top hat in his hands, squashing it, and looked overwhelmed at the group of people that surrounded him. When he saw Birdie, he started, paled, took several steps forward, paused, a look of uneasiness crossing his face.

"This gentleman here insists he is your husband," said Henry, the Duke of Ashmore in a languid tone. "I find this rather perplexing, as I was not aware that you were married, to begin with."

"Certainly, we are married," Gabriel insisted.

"The marriage isn't valid," Birdie muttered afterwards. She clasped her hands together tightly.

"No doubt you will decide in your own time whether you are indeed married, or not," Ashmore said, with twitching lips.

"Excuse me. But who are you?" Gabriel looked at him, pulling together his brows. The butler had announced him, but none of the present people had introduced themselves so far.

"Oh, stop teasing the poor man, Henry," Lucy chastised her husband. She turned to Gabriel with a smile. "This is my husband, the Duke of Ashmore. Never mind him. His bark is worse than his bite. I am Lucy, Birdie's dear friend. I am pleased to meet you, despite your unfortunate tendency to lock yourself up in fairy tale towers. This is Arabella, my sister-in-law, and the children screeching on the lawn are her stepchildren, Robin and Joy. Although I daresay the one screeching the loudest is my own offspring. The lady in the chair is the dowager duchess Augusta. We will let her sleep. And this, of course, is Birdie. She has been expecting you." She drew a reluctant Birdie forward.

"But Lucy..." Now that he was here, the last thing Birdie wanted to do was talk to him. Especially not alone.

His eyes bore into hers.

She stared wordlessly across at him, her heart pounding.

"I would like to talk to my wife alone." It sounded more like a command, not a request, in the kind of tone that he'd use with his soldiers.

The Duke of Ashmore, no doubt unused to being commanded about in his own home, lifted an unamused eyebrow. To anyone in the ton, that would've been a sign that the recipient had just been socially exterminated. Gabriel, however, was happily unaware of that and lifted an eyebrow at the duke in return. Given that he had only one, it made a ferocious impact.

Birdie felt Lucy's hand upon her back, pushing her towards Gabriel and she stalled.

Arabella, more perceptive, looked at Birdie with a worried frown.

Ashmore was equally perceptive. "My dear Duke. What you want or not is entirely beside the point. The question, rather is, what does the lady want, and is she inclined to talk with you?"

Birdie decided she liked Lucy's husband immensely. She threw him a grateful look.

"I'd rather not," she said. "I mean, I am certain there is not much to discuss." She waved a hand dismissively. "I mean, what is there to say? Certainly nothing from my side. If you have something to say, you can say it here."

"You can't mean that," Gabriel said roughly.

Birdie could be stubborn when she wanted to. She pushed out her lower lip and evaded his look. Her heart hammered. There was nothing she could tell him. She had told him her story; she had asked for his forgiveness; she knew she didn't deserve it. She would not beg for his love. Maybe he would leave now and then she could continue nursing her wounded heart. She heard him breathe heavily. Then sigh.

When she heard Arabella and Lucy gasp in unison, her eyes flew up—and she froze.

In the Duke of Ashmore's drawing room, Captain Eversleigh, also known as the Duke of Dunross, who'd lived as a hermit in a stone tower the last five years and who'd eschewed society as best as he could, had got down on his knees in front of the entire company.

"I am not a man of many words, and when I do speak, I have no pretty words to offer," he began. "I am a simple man, a soldier, who knows only how to get things done by commanding other men across the battlefield. I would beg your forgiveness for not having listened to reason when you tried to explain your situation to me. My only excuse is that I was overwhelmed with the events that had happened. McKenna's death. The smuggling. Your brother's arrival. I really did not know what to think anymore. I just wanted you to know that I have sought out Cecily Burns. She is Mrs Cecily Varns now, as she has married the vicar's son, and both seem to be very happy. I had a good talk with both, and her account of events is identical to yours. Not that I needed that confirmation, but she insisted that it had been all her idea and that she alone was to blame. She considers you her saviour and insists that she would have never found her happiness if it hadn't been for you. I have settled a good portion of my pension on her, so Cecily and her family will be provided for, and with that, I consider my vow to her father fulfilled. I then visited Miss Hilversham's Seminary, and I was devastated not to find you there. The good lady sent me here. Please tell me I have not come in vain. I need you to know one thing: that I love you dearly, with all my heart and soul and all I am capable of. I have done so from the moment you returned to the church, with the lightning flashing all about you. You looked like a fairy tale creature, magical and beautiful. I did not realise the truth about my emotions until you left. I am, undoubtedly, a fool. Even if you find you cannot reciprocate the feeling, I beg you to accept my humble hand in marriage. Allow me to make amends."

Gabriel let out a sigh as he concluded his speech. His eyes filled with tears; he was evidently in agony.

Everyone in the room remained still. They could hear the ormolu clock ticking in the silence.

Gabriel remained on his knees. Everyone turned to stare at Birdie.

"Of course, she will accept you!" Lucy bounced up and down on the sofa.

"Hush, Lucy, let Birdie speak for herself," Arabella interrupted and wrung her hands.

"If the obvious answer doesn't immediately come to her, then—" Ashmore contributed.

Birdie choked forth a sob and threw herself at Gabriel. In an attempt to hold her, he nearly fell backwards. "Oh, I do, I do, I do, how can you even ask, you silly man. I've loved you so, every minute and I felt so damned that I did, knowing it was all a lie and that you were not really mine." Birdie sobbed into his waistcoat.

Gabriel clutched her to him tightly as an incredulous smile spread over his face.

Lucy and Arabella cried along. "That was the most romantic speech I've ever heard." Arabella wiped her nose. "Philip wasn't nearly as romantic."

"Nor was Henry," Lucy said.

Ashmore cleared his throat.

"Oh, my love, I dared not hope. Not after all you've gone through. I would like to kiss you, but blast it, can I do this without an audience?"

"Well, there it is. I will seek Morley. Where the deuce has the fellow disappeared to?" Ashmore fled through the veranda door.

Gabriel must have decided that waiting until everyone had left was too long to bear, so he kissed Birdie right there and then.

The dowager duchess woke up with an abrupt snore. "Did I miss something?"

Lucy clapped her hands. "Oh, how wonderful! We will have a wedding here, yes? Did you get a special license, Duke?"

Gabriel nodded. "I did, indeed. As Miss Hilversham kept

insisting that our wedding might not be valid, I decided not to leave things up to chance. Even if it is a valid marriage, I was thinking there is no harm in being married again, properly." He looked down tenderly on Birdie. "With your friends and with everything that a proper wedding ought to include."

"Wedding? Most irksome to take a nap and to find, upon one's awakening, that the entire house is in the middle of wedding preparations. I vow I shall never nap again." The dowager duchess sniffed.

"Birdie is marrying her duke for the second time. Isn't it wonderful, grandmamma? I will tell you all about it. We will have to start preparations immediately, won't we, Arabella?" Lucy bustled to the door, dragging Arabella with her. She opened it and stood face to face with Philip, who took a startled step backwards.

"Dash it, I've been looking for Ashmore but can't find the fellow. I've had the most sudden inspiration for an amendment to the transportation device that I think will be more amenable, with different technology, not the hydraulic power—" Philip Merivale, Duke of Morley, cut himself short, and gaped at Gabriel. "But—Sir! Captain! Captain Eversleigh! Am I dreaming?"

Then Philip did the oddest thing: he gave a military salute. Gabriel, however, had turned a deathly shade of pale.

"Merivale. This cannot be. For you are dead!"

CHAPTER 25

"He is very much alive and breathing." Arabella drew her dazed husband forward. "I should know best, because I'm married to him."

"I saw you fall at Hougoumont. A cannon. Your head—" Gabriel breathed heavily. "I was the only one in my company to survive after Napoleon ordered the shelling of the place."

"Sir! My head is safe and sound on my shoulders, sir. I believed you to be dead, sir. I was told everyone fell in battle, save for myself." Philip looked dazed.

Could it be possible? But he'd seen it so clearly. One moment the man had stood next to him, the other, he'd been gone. Merivale, one of his best men, supremely intelligent, father of two children and a third on the way. Had he imagined it all? He'd mourned him like no other. Gabriel reached out for Philip's hand and pumped it.

"In the general chaos of the battle, it would've been easy to confuse things. Especially if you, yourself, were wounded as well." Birdie stepped up to them.

"I have never been happier to see a man alive," Philip said shakily, and clapped Gabriel's shoulder. Gabriel clapped him back, and in the general shoulder clapping process, clearing of throats, and blinking back of tears, the dowager duchess' voice intruded grumpily:

"Well, wonderful. Now that we have firmly established that neither man is a ghost, may we proceed to have some tea?" She thumped her stick on the floor impatiently.

THE WEDDING in the Ashmore chapel was a simple, but lovely affair. Birdie wore a dress of cream and gold, with a gauze overdress, gloves and a pretty bonnet adorned with Ashmore's roses. Philip had insisted on being the one to give the bride away. As Birdie walked down the aisle on his arm, she beamed at her friends, who sat in the pews, moist-eyed and smiled back tremulously. She felt she was in a dream. Could anyone be as happy as she?

Gabriel gazed at her from the altar with such a look of love in his eyes that she fairly choked up.

The reverend, an elderly man with a shock of white hair, stood in front of the altar and looked at them both benevolently when Birdie reached Gabriel's side. "Dearly beloved. We are gathered here today—" he began.

"Stop!" Birdie interrupted hastily.

A gasp went through the chapel. The reverend gaped.

Turning to Gabriel, Birdie said, "We need to say our vows properly. Remember?"

Gabriel pressed her hand and smiled down at her. "You are entirely right." He took Birdie's hands in his and turned to face the congregation. "I would like everyone who has gathered here to witness that I will love, obey, respect, serve, comfort and care for this wonderful woman, my very own Roberta Talbot, through all the days of my life," he declared.

Birdie smiled up at him tremulously. "I will love you today, tomorrow, and forevermore through easy and difficult days," she said. "I will trust and honour you, laugh and cry with you, and whatever may come, I will always be there for you."

The reverend, somewhat amused by this unorthodox ceremony, closed his Bible and beamed at the couple. "I now pronounce you man and wife."

Birdie lifted her mouth to his. Gabriel lowered his lips, warm and sweet on hers.

Her entire being filled with fierce happiness knowing that they were meant for each other.

EPILOGUE

ASHMORE HALL, OXFORDSHIRE, 1820

"*D*o stay longer, Birdie!" Lucy pestered her friend. "Philip and Arabella and the children will be here; Katy is coming from the seminary, and you haven't even met her, have you? And we will have such fun together. Oh, do persuade your husband to stay."

Birdie hesitated. While she loved the idea of visiting longer with her friends, she also yearned for more time alone with her husband.

The change that had gone through him the last few months was astounding. No longer the reserved, antisocial hermit, he'd turned into an astoundingly talkative socialite who discussed in detail every move and manoeuvre of the Napoleonic wars, most frequently with Philip, who joined in with equal enthusiasm. They were caught up in a string of "Do you remember when?" and discussed every single battle they'd been in together.

After Gabriel had mentioned he'd created a model of the

battle, Philip had been eager to create a similar one—right here and right now.

Even more astounding, the Duke of Ashmore had allowed himself to get drawn into the project as well. It appeared he regretted not having been able to join the war. But through his readings of newspapers and discussions with war veterans, he had accumulated a sound basis of knowledge on the Peninsula wars. The three men were inseparable, as they planned on how to build a model that would be three times the size of what Gabriel had in his castle in Scotland. Parts of it would move on their own, Philip had vowed.

After tea, Birdie drew Gabriel aside.

He was reading a missive. "You won't believe this, Birdie," he started. "But your brother, it appears, really knows his business when it comes to whisky production."

Birdie had been sceptical about Freddie's involvement in the business, but as it had been his idea to begin with, and as anything that he did that was not gambling was to be approved of, she decided to go along with it.

"Merivale—that is, Morley—I can never call him like that, can I? He will always be Merivale to me—has said he can come up with a process that will speed up the production. In fact, he's suggested to return with us to Scotland. What do you say to that?"

"Oh, Gabriel, that would be wonderful! Arabella is to come with him?"

"As well as the children, it seems." Gabriel grinned. He was the Merivale children's favourite person. After an initial shocked glance at his cheek and the expected questions surrounding the injury and whether it still hurt awfully, they soon decided Gabriel was a grand sport. Especially if he was to build another model, as he promised, specifically for them to play with.

"I hate to interrupt you lovebirds," Lucy said as she

approached them, a troubled look on her face. "I need to talk to Birdie." She also motioned Arabella to follow her to another room.

The three women left together and bustled into an adjacent room.

"What has happened? You look troubled," Birdie asked.

Lucy handed her a letter wordlessly. It was from Miss Hilversham. Her normally neat and legible handwriting was almost undecipherable.

Birdie read through it and gasped. "It's Pen! She's run away!"

Arabella clasped her hand over her heart. "Oh! I seem to have set a terrible precedence. First Birdie, now Pen."

"It's me. I started it all." Lucy wrung her hands. "I somehow put the idea in your heads, didn't I?"

"Where is she?" Birdie asked.

"She's gone to London. Alone. That is all Miss Hilversham knows."

Birdie closed her eyes. "She has gone after that man. Her guardian."

Arabella gasped. "Are you certain?"

Birdie nodded. "We shared a room, didn't we? She wouldn't stop talking about him. You know, there was a time when I thought she'd invented him? He never showed his face. He never came to the seminary. I was certain he never existed."

"You're right. He never came to visit her, not once. Nor was she invited to spend the holidays with him. What kind of guardian is that?"

"Yet he paid for her tuition, and once a letter arrived."

"She slept with the letter under the pillow for half a year."

Birdie tapped a finger against the letter. "I believe she was —possibly still is—head over heels in love with him." Her eyes widened as she realised something. "I also believe he was the reason she wanted to retrieve the coin from the wishing well that night."

Indeed, the night Arabella had thrown in four coins to the wishing well, wishing for a Duke for each girl to marry, Pen had become upset and insisted on retrieving one coin—her coin—from the well.

She'd fallen in with a crash, dragging Arabella down with her.

The women fell silent as they all recollected that.

Arabella turned to Birdie with fear in her eyes. "What are you saying? That she doesn't want to marry a duke because—"

"Because she is in love with someone who is *not* a duke," Birdie and Lucy said simultaneously.

"And now she's run off to London to find him."

The girls stared at each other wordlessly.

IN THE DEPTHS of the turquoise waters of the wishing well in Paradise Row, a single coin glittered.

DON'T MISS Penelope's and Alworth's story in *Penelope and the Wicked Duke!*

ABOUT THE AUTHOR

Sofi was born in Vienna, grew up in Seoul, studied Comparative Literature in Maryland, U.S.A., and lived in Quito with her Ecuadorian husband. When not writing, she likes to scramble about the countryside exploring medieval castle ruins. She currently lives with her husband, 3 trilingual children, a sassy cat, and a cheeky dog in Europe.

Get in touch and visit Sofi at her Website, on Facebook or Instagram!

facebook.com/sofilaporteauthor
instagram.com/sofilaporteauthor
amazon.com/Sofi-Laporte/e/B07N1K8H6C
bookbub.com/profile/sofi-laporte